LUCY

Animal Ark™

Sheepdog
in the
Snow

Hodder
Children's
Books

A division of Hachette Children's Books

Special thanks to Jenny Oldfield
Thanks also to C. J. Hall, B.Vet.Med., M.R.C.V.S., for reviewing the
veterinary information contained in this book

Animal Ark is a trademark of Working Partners Ltd
Text copyright © Ben M. Baglio 1995
Created by Ben M. Baglio, London W6 0HE
Illustrations copyright © Shelagh McNicholas 1995

First published in Great Britain in 1995
by Hodder Children's Books
This edition published in 2007

The right of Lucy Daniels to be identified as the author of
this work has been asserted by her in accordance with the
Copyright, Designs and Patents Act 1988.

1

A Catalogue record for this book is available from the British Library

ISBN-13: 978 0 340 94537 7

Typeset in Baskerville by Avon DataSet Ltd,
Bidford-on-Avon, Warwickshire

Printed and bound in Great Britain by
Clays Ltd, St Ives plc

The paper and board used in this paperback by Hodder Children's
Books are natural recyclable products made from wood grown in
sustainable forests. The manufacturing processes conform to the
environmental regulations of the country of origin.

Hodder Children's Books
a division of Hachette Children's Books
338 Euston Road, London NW1 3BH
An Hachette Livre UK company

To the real Tess

One

Christmas was coming. Mandy Hope's school had broken up for the holidays. Brightly wrapped presents were stacked under the tree in the cosy kitchen at Animal Ark, and Mandy and her friend, James Hunter, were hunched over the table surrounded by invitation cards.

'Let's make a list,' James suggested. He chewed the end of his pen. 'In alphabetical order.'

'What kind of list?' Mandy pushed her blonde hair behind her ears and scribbled away. She was making out an invitation to Gran and Granded Hope, and Smoky the cat. Each card was hand-designed by James and Mandy. They'd cut out squares of bright yellow card, drawn the black outline of a Christmas tree on to each one, and written the words 'PARTY TIME' across the top.

'A list of guests.' James liked to be organised. He didn't want to miss anyone out. He saw Mandy was rushing into things a bit too fast. 'Shall we put pets or people first?'

'Pets,' came the prompt reply. Mandy filled out her grandparents' card. 'A Christmas Eve Party!' it read. 'Pets, bring your owners to Welford Village Hall on Saturday, 24 December at 7.30 p.m. Music and Food!' It was signed with a miniature cat's paw print, from a stencil which James had made.

'OK.' James began his list. 'Barney and Button . . . Blackie . . . Dorian . . . Eric . . . Houdini . . .' He ran through the names of some of the pets they'd helped in the past. 'Rosa won't be able to come because she's hibernating . . . but Sammy probably will, because squirrels only semi-hibernate, and—'

'Hang on a second; you missed out Ruby and Prince.' Mandy remembered the piglet and the pony as she tucked the invitation into an envelope.

'Hmm . . . Can we get a pony into the village hall?' James wondered.

Mandy thought carefully. 'I suppose Susan could

bring him and stay outside with him. Prince could stick his head through an open window and enjoy things from there.'

'And what about pigs?'

She imagined cheeky, adventurous Ruby trotting in and out of the trestle-tables, rooting for food. She nodded. 'Pigs are fine. We want everyone to come, remember. It's going to be the biggest, best Christmas party for pets anyone's ever seen!'

Mandy's blue eyes shone. Animals were the love of her life, and the idea of giving them a Christmas treat, where all the past patients of Animal Ark could get together with pets which Mandy and James had helped to rescue, and farm animals they'd managed to save, promised to make this a Christmas to remember.

She imagined everyone gathered there; cats and dogs, rabbits, hamsters, sheep and pigs. She wanted to invite Ernie Bell and his squirrel, Sammy, Lydia Fawcett and her wonderful escaping goat, Houdini. She even wanted Pandora the Pekinese and Toby the mongrel, though this would mean having to invite their fussy owner, Mrs Ponsonby. 'I wonder if Pandora will come in fancy dress?' Mandy smiled.

'No, but I expect Mrs Ponsonby will.' James

hitched his glasses further up his nose. He slotted Pandora's name into the list. 'Hey, let's have a competition for the best party hat!' he suggested.

'And carols. And a Christmas procession down the village street.' Mandy could picture the magic scene. For a few moments she stopped to daydream. She'd take along Mopsy, the tamest of her three rabbits, warmly zipped up inside the front of her jacket. They would have to draw up a menu of food, from lettuce leaves for Mopsy to oats for Susan Price's pony. It would be snowing outside, and they would carry candles down the street. They would crowd into the village hall, singing carols. Then the pets would be let loose on the party food . . .

'Mandy?' James broke in.

'Hmm?'

'I said, do you want to invite Imogen with Button and Barney, or John Hardy?'

'Both,' Mandy beamed. She was feeling generous. 'You know, Imogen Parker Smythe isn't nearly so spoiled now she has the two rabbits to look after. In fact, I'd even say she was quite nice!'

'And what about Claire?' James remembered his little, dark-haired, next-door neighbour. She ran a hedgehog sanctuary in her garden. 'Rosa, Guy and everyone will be fast asleep for the winter in their nest-boxes.'

Mandy's brow wrinkled. 'Yes, we can't wake them up specially, just to come to a party. Claire will have to come by herself.' She began to make out a fresh invitation. It was only five days until Christmas Eve, and they had loads to do.

In the background, they could hear Adam Hope, Mandy's dad, pottering about the house. He went up and downstairs, in and out of the lounge, humming and singing to himself. Then he put his bearded face round the kitchen door.

Christmas is coming,
The goose is getting fat . . .

he sang;

Please put a penny
In the old man's hat.
If you haven't got a penny,
A halfpenny will do.
If you haven't got a halfpenny,
A farthing will do.
If you haven't got a farthing . . .

'*God bless you!*' Mandy and James chimed in, their faces wreathed in smiles.

'Busy?' Mr Hope asked. He picked up an invitation card. 'Good idea,' he nodded. 'Yes. Pets at a party, very good. A get-together, hmm . . .' He wandered off again, grabbing his white coat from the back of a chair. Then he headed off to the Animal Ark surgery in the modern extension at the back of their old stone cottage. They heard him 'pom-pom-pom'ing on an imaginary trombone as he went.

Mandy grinned at James. She loved her absent-minded, easy-going dad, and she thought his job as a vet in Animal Ark was the best there was. And when she grew up, she wanted to be a vet herself.

'What about Simon and Jean?' James thought of the veterinary nurse and receptionist. 'They don't have anyone to bring. Pets, I mean.'

'They can come anyway.' Mandy watched James add them to the list. She jumped up from the table, uncurling her fingers and stretching her arms. 'I've got writer's cramp,' she said. 'How about going to ask Simon and Jean right now?'

James didn't need a second prompting. He liked the surgery, its reception area crowded out during surgery hours with animal patients; hairy and sleek, big and tiny, noisy and silent. He was out of his seat and through the door before Mandy had finished stretching. He headed for the extension and its miaowing, shuffling, snuffling queue.

James and Mandy rushed in to say hello to the people and pets they knew from the village and farms surrounding Welford. They noticed Jack Spiller, with his daughter, Jenny, and their old sheepdog. They worked on a smallholding out of town. The dog had scratched her eye and it was infected, Jack said. He kept a close watch on Sam Western, who was also in the surgery with his new dog; a large German shepherd, mostly black, with a pale brown face and chest. He was a fine animal, but edgy by the look of him. Sam Western didn't keep his dogs up at Upper Welford Hall as pets, but as guard dogs to see off trespassers. Mandy bent to talk gently to the nervous animal. 'What's his name?' she asked Mr Western.

'Major.' The reply was brisk. Mr Western looked impatiently at his watch. 'How much longer?' he asked Jean Knox.

The grey-haired receptionist checked the appointment book. 'You're next, Mr Western. It shouldn't be long now.'

'They're running five minutes late in there,' he

complained. Sam Western was a busy and important man and he liked everyone to know it.

Mandy smiled and stroked Major, then she and James approached the reception desk.

'What are you doing this Saturday, Jean?' Mandy leaned both elbows on the counter.

'Let's see, Saturday? Why, that's Christmas Eve, isn't it?' Jean counted out the days on her fingers. 'As a matter of fact, I don't have anything planned.' She peered at them over her glasses.

'Would you like to come to a party at the village hall?' James asked. 'It's for everyone from Animal Ark and their owners.'

Jean took off her glasses and put her head to one side. 'Shouldn't that be "everyone and their *pets?*" '

'No, it's a *pets*' party,' Mandy insisted. 'But there'll be food and drink for people too.' She felt grateful that her mum and Mrs Hunter, James's mum, had both agreed to contribute towards the cost. 'We'd like everyone to come.'

'Well, I suppose I could fit in making my mince pies earlier in the day. And I go to midnight mass, but that's much later, of course. Yes, I'd be delighted, thank you!' She beamed at them and began searching the counter. 'Let me write that down!'

'Here's a pen.' James handed her one. 'It begins at seven-thirty.'

Jean took the pen and looked helplessly for a spare scrap of paper.

'Here!' Mandy took one from her pocket. 'And your glasses are round your neck.' She was used to helping their receptionist find the things she'd lost.

Jean smiled again as she fixed them on her nose. 'Ah, thank you, Mandy dear.' She looked across the room as the surgery door opened. Walter Pickard emerged with his elderly cat, Tom. 'Mr Western, you can take Major in now.'

Mandy went up to her old friend, Walter, who lived in the row of small cottages beside the Fox and Goose. 'What's Tom been up to?' She tickled the cat's chin. 'His ear's in a bit of a state, isn't it?'

'He's been in a scrap,' the old man grumbled. 'You'd think he'd know better.'

Burly Tom looked as if he couldn't care less. Bitten ear or not, the next chance he got, he'd be scrapping again. He purred proudly as Mandy inspected his chewed ear.

They stood to one side as Mr Western pushed past towards the treatment room. He held Major on a short lead, but the dog managed to lift his head and growl at old Tom.

Simon stood at the door, waiting. When he spotted Mandy, he spoke rapidly. 'Grab a white coat and give me a hand in here, would you? We're a bit behind.' He smiled at Mr Western and escorted him into the small, clean, white room.

'Is that OK?' Mandy checked with James.

He nodded. 'I'll go and do some more invitations. We'd better get up to High Cross later today, to call in on Lydia and on the Parker Smythes.'

Mandy agreed. 'I won't be long,' she promised.

Inside the treatment room, Simon had already lifted the big German shepherd dog on to the table. Mr Western stood against the wall. The dog's ears were laid flat, its teeth bared. But Simon dealt with him expertly and calmly, stroking his long back and encouraging him to stand still. 'This is a magnificent animal you have here, Mr Western,' he said. 'Where did you get him?'

'From a house in York. Small garden. Hopeless.' Mr Western didn't smile. He used words sparingly, as if they cost money.

'No good at all for a chap this size,' Simon agreed. 'You need plenty of space to run around in, don't you, boy?' He inspected the dog's ears and

gently eased open his jaw. 'He's not been ill-treated, at least.'

Mr Western grunted. 'He just needs his injections. I don't want him keeling over on me, not after what I've just paid for him. And I don't want him infecting the other two dogs either.'

Mandy frowned and went to a drawer to fetch rubber gloves and a syringe pack for Simon, while the nurse took the drugs from a high, locked cupboard. Mr Western owned a large estate on the moorside. He was a dairy farmer, using modern methods, but, strangely, he didn't seem to like animals. He was stocky and bad-tempered, and ran his place strictly. Mandy imagined a stern, open-air life for Major from now on, after his cooped-up existence in the city.

Simon spoke soothingly to the dog, while Mandy stood at his head, holding his collar firmly. He jerked as Simon made the injection, and his back legs shifted, but he gave no other sign. 'That's it; good boy,' Simon said. Mandy let him jump easily to the floor.

Quickly Mr Western hooked the dog's lead back on. 'That's it; you've finished?' he asked. Simon nodded. With a curt 'thank you', the farmer left the room. 'Put this down on my account,' he told Jean. Soon the outer doors were swinging behind him and his new guard dog.

'Simon!' Mandy found time for a quiet word before the next patient came in. She'd disposed of the gloves and syringe in a special sealed bin. 'Are you doing anything on Christmas Eve?' She prayed he could come to their party. He could bring his music collection and be the disc jockey.

'Not much so far.' When he heard Mandy's offer, he said he'd love to come.

She smiled. *So far, so good*, she thought.

Then it was time to get busy again, tending to a wounded rabbit's paw, innoculating another dog, strapping up a kitten's sprained back leg.

Time flew. Before Mandy knew it, morning surgery was over and she was free to go back to James and the party preparations.

Two

By midday, Mandy and James had gathered their pile of carefully named envelopes, put them into their coat pockets, and set off on their bikes for High Cross. It was a clear, sunny Monday as they cycled down the drive from Animal Ark, under the wooden sign swinging in the cold wind. As far as the eye could see, down the valley to the riverside, and up the steep, soaring moorside to the Beacon and High Cross Farm, the air was crisp and bright. The trees stood grey and bare. The hills were a range of dull browns and sharp greens.

Mandy's breath clouded the freezing air. She pedalled hard to get warm. Soon, she and James were cycling through the village, up the main street, past the Fox and Goose, the church and the village hall, where their great event was to take place.

Their first stop was Bleakfell Hall, Mrs Ponsonby's grand house just outside the village. 'Might as well get this over with,' Mandy sighed, knowing that Mrs Ponsonby would go on and on about poor Pandora's latest mystery ailment. Even though Pandora was perfectly healthy, Mrs Ponsonby seemed to bring the Pekinese to Animal Ark virtually every week. Mandy swung open the gate, and together she and James cycled up the drive.

The front door opened, and Pandora and Toby came flying out of the house to greet them, yapping and jumping up in pleasure.

'Down, Toby, down!' Mrs Ponsonby scolded. She followed them out, wearing a pink flowered apron over her royal blue dress. Her round plump face was set off by pink winged glasses with a sparkling diamante decoration. She ignored the fact that her beloved Pandora was gnawing at James's trouser leg, and bore down instead on poor Toby. 'Bad boy, down!'

Mandy smiled at the friendly mongrel and told him to sit. Toby obliged. His tail wagged to and fro against the gravel drive. Mandy put down her bike, pulled out Mrs Ponsonby's invitation and handed it to her.

'What's this?' she exclaimed. She tore open the envelope in great excitement. 'Oh, a party!' she read. Then her face changed. She frowned. 'What's this? A party for pets? Oh no; I don't think so, my dear.' She shook her head.

'Why not?' Mandy looked in dismay at Pandora and Toby.

Mrs Ponsonby creaked forward to scoop up a dog under each arm. 'Pandora's not very strong, you see. A party would be too much for her. I'm afraid I shall have to say no.'

Pandora whined and wheezed.

'What about Toby?' James stood astride his bike, inspecting the small holes in the leg of his jeans.

'Toby can't go without his best friend, Pandora, can you, Toby-Woby?' Mrs Ponsonby made squeaking noises with her lips. 'That wouldn't be fair on Pandy-Wandy, now would it?' She glanced up at Mandy. 'I'm afraid we shall have to decline your kind offer.'

Mandy swallowed hard. It was a shame that the two pets would miss out. She knew for a fact that Pandora was as tough as the next dog; it was only Mrs Ponsonby's fussy nature that made her see death and disaster round every corner. 'I'm sorry you can't

come.' She picked up her bike and leaned forward
to give the dogs a pat.

For a moment, Mrs Ponsonby seemed to be about
to change her mind. 'I suppose your mother and
father will be there to supervise?' She tried to sound
casual. 'And your grandparents?'

Mandy nodded. 'I've already asked Gran
unofficially. She's promised to help with the food.'

This seemed unwelcome news to Mrs Ponsonby.
She stepped back and sniffed. 'Really? Has Dorothy
asked for permission?'

Mandy remembered, too late, that bossy Mrs
Ponsonby and Gran rarely saw eye to eye. They both
loved to organise, but neither liked to take orders
from the other. 'What for?' she asked.

'To take food into the village hall. You must ask
the vicar's permission, you know. It's a church hall,
after all. In fact, Reverend Hadcroft is rather
particular about it. He doesn't like a mess.'

'Oh. I'll check,' Mandy said flatly. She put it to the
top of her list of things to do. 'Let's go and ask Gran
about it,' she said to James with a worried look. It
was too late to change the party venue now, with
Christmas Eve only five days away and the invitations
already written out . . .

* * *

'Take no notice of Mrs Ponsonby,' said Gran.

Mandy and James had cycled straight back to Lilac Cottage. 'She's only trying to throw a spanner in the works.' Her eyes sparkled and she spoke firmly. 'It's because you asked *me* to help with the food, you see. Amelia Ponsonby can't bear anyone else to do the organising. Now, if you'd asked *her*, my dear, I'm sure that she would have turned around and decided that Pandora was as fit as a fiddle after all, and she'd be down at the village hall right this minute, buttering mountains of sliced bread for sandwiches.'

Mandy grinned with relief.

'No, don't worry. Reverend Hadcroft won't mind in the least little bit. And life will be quieter without Mrs Ponsonby breathing down our necks!'

'It's a pity about Toby and Pandora, though,' James said wistfully, as they rode up the hill towards High Cross at last. 'And all because Mrs Ponsonby doesn't get to make the sandwiches.'

They had to stop talking to concentrate on the steep climb. It made them hot and breathless, even on this crisp winter's day. When they reached the top and stopped beside some big iron gates, they saw the Parker Smythe mansion locked up, with no cars in the drive. James went to slip Imogen's invitation through the letter-box. Then they were on their way again, past Sam Western's barking dogs in the grounds of his huge farm, on to the small stone farmhouse at the end of the track. It stood almost in the shadow of the ancient Celtic monument; Lydia Fawcett's goat farm, High Cross.

As she heard them approach, gentle, shy Lydia came out of the barn. She was dressed in her old brown work coat and wellingtons. She smiled as she strode to meet them, leading high-stepping Houdini. The black and white goat had a wicked light in his eye and snickered a greeting. Mandy ran up and gave him a hug. 'How would you like to come to a Christmas party, Houdini?' she asked.

'And you too, Lydia.' James handed her the invitation.

Lydia umed and aahed. She wasn't a party sort of person. She had her goats to look after. She didn't get down to the village much during these dark evenings.

'But it's Christmas Eve!' Mandy protested. She knew that Lydia didn't drive a car. 'Listen, I'm sure I can get my dad to drive up in the Land-rover and fetch you and Houdini, and bring you safely back again. He wouldn't mind!'

Lydia blushed, and though she said she wouldn't

dream of putting Mr Hope out in that way, she gradually gave way to her friends' pleas. 'Ernie will be there with Sammy,' James promised. 'You'll know loads of people. Please come, Lydia!'

Houdini nodded his head impatiently. They all laughed at him. 'Very well,' Lydia said at last. 'Mind you, I haven't any pretty party dresses.'

'Come as you are,' Mandy smiled. 'Just as long as you come!'

They waved and rode off down the track, pleased with their success at persuading their shy friend and their favourite goat.

'Where to next?' James asked. They sped along the high moor road. The village nestled in the valley bottom. They could see for miles.

'Ernie and Sammy's?' Mandy suggested. 'Since we've already told Lydia they'll be there!' It was a white lie, and all in a good cause.

James agreed. Ernie Bell had built the strong fences to keep Lydia's goats safely penned in. The two were good company for one another; Ernie was always less grumpy when Lydia was around, and Lydia was less shy. 'Let's hope he says yes,' he said. Besides, Sammy the squirrel was one of his favourite pets.

But they'd only cycled a few more metres before a

movement on the winding road ahead caught Mandy's eye. She braked and waited for the shape to reappear out of a hollow. It was heading slowly in their direction.

'What's wrong?' James slowed down beside her.

'I think there's an animal on the road.' Mandy glanced round for traffic danger, but the exposed moor road was deserted. 'There it is again, look!' She pointed. A black creature came up the hill.

'It's a dog.' James saw it too. 'I think it's limping.'

Quickly Mandy lay down her bike against the grass verge. 'Don't scare it. Let's wait here.' What was a dog doing in the middle of nowhere on a cold, raw day like this?

James and Mandy stood waiting for the dog to approach. It came with a halting step, its left front paw so sore that it could scarcely touch the ground.

'It looks like some kind of sheepdog,' James whispered. 'Do you think it's lost?'

Mandy shook her head. 'I don't know. It's not from round here, though. At least, I don't recognise it.'

The dog limped along. Its head hung low, its tongue lolled, its tail brushed the ground. The wind blew in its face as it mounted the hill, slowing it almost to a standstill.

'Poor thing!' Mandy's heart went out at once to

the suffering creature. She saw it was female. 'Look how thin she is!' She squatted down and beckoned the dog. 'Here, girl, here!'

The dog lifted her dull head and caught sight of them at last. She halted, too weary to avoid them by heading off across the verge and over the low stone wall into the field beyond. She whined and hung her head.

'She must be starving!' James knelt down at Mandy's side. 'Here, girl. Look, she's not wearing a collar or a name-tag. Goodness knows how far she's walked.'

Mandy sighed. 'Who's left her here?' Again, she scanned the countryside, but there was no sign of an owner, either in a car or on foot.

Eventually the dog seemed strong enough to resume her limping progress. She moved forward. Close to, they could see that her black coat was matted, the underside of her long tail tangled with mud and thorns. Her front paws, speckled grey and white, were a dull, muddy brown. Worst of all, her thin sides heaved with the effort of hauling herself up the long hill. Through her coat, they could see the shape of her ribcage, and the lean, starved haunches.

'Poor thing!' Mandy gasped again. The dog came

alongside, head down, trying to creep quietly by. But her injured paw hit against a small rock at the roadside. She yelped and staggered sideways towards them. Mandy and James ran forward to help.

The dog whined, her sides heaved, and she fell at their feet. She lay on her side, eyes and mouth open, tongue lolling. Gently, Mandy put out a hand to stroke her head. The deep brown eyes stared back.

'There, girl, there.' Mandy felt like crying for the wounded, starved animal. She looked up at James with tears in her eyes. 'We've got to get her back to Welford!' she whispered. 'Let's get her to Animal Ark.'

'She's nearly dead, poor thing!' James warned Mandy to be gentle.

The dog lay in the road. She made one sad attempt to wag her tail in greeting, as if she knew that these were her rescuers. She gave herself up to James and Mandy's care, closed her eyes and slipped gently into unconsciousness.

Three

Quickly, Mandy unzipped her warm woollen jacket and wrapped the dog inside it. 'I'll leave my bike here,' she told James. 'Can you go ahead and tell Mum and Dad what's happening?' Ever so gently, she edged her arms under the limp body and lifted it from the cold ground.

'Are you sure you can carry her?' James stood astride his bike, his face pale and worried.

She nodded. 'I'll manage. Get someone to bring the car out. Hurry, please!' Steadying herself, she began to carry the dog down the hill.

James set off, crouched over his handlebars, speeding into the dip, pedalling for all he was worth up the other side. He was soon out of sight.

Mandy trudged on. The dog didn't weigh much, even wrapped inside Mandy's coat. She was mostly skin and bone, but she heaved a sigh and her eyelids fluttered. Mandy spoke gently to her as she walked. 'There, girl, there. We'll soon have you back safe and sound.' Inside her head, another voice whispered, *Let's hope we're not too late!*

Several minutes passed. Still Mandy walked on towards Welford. Only one car passed her, travelling in the other direction. Two curious faces looked out, but the car roared by.

Mandy's arms began to ache. The dog was a dead weight, cradled against her chest.

At last she caught sight of the Animal Ark Land-rover speeding along the road towards her, her mum at the wheel. As the car pulled up, Mandy gave a gasp of relief. 'Oh Mum, thank heavens!'

Emily Hope and James leaped out. Mrs Hope hurried across and took a quick glance at the unconscious sheepdog. She ran back for her bag. 'Bring her over here as quick as you can,' she told Mandy, flinging open the back door. 'Lay her down. That's right. Now stand back and let me take a proper look.'

Mandy put the poor creature into the back of the car. She straightened up and peered anxiously over her mother's shoulder, knowing that if anyone could save the dog, Emily Hope could.

'She's badly dehydrated,' Mrs Hope said, after pinching a bit of the dog's skin. 'Now James, pass me that glucose solution. That's the one.' She made sure the dog stayed warmly wrapped inside the jacket, then she lifted her head and offered a few drops of the sweet liquid by mouth, through a syringe feed. They saw the dog's throat constrict and swallow. Her pink tongue passed across her lips. Mrs Hope gave her a few drops more. Soon her eyes opened and she was licking and swallowing greedily.

Mandy looked across at James. She sighed. Mrs Hope stroked the dog's throat to help her swallow. They saw the tip of her tail wag free of her makeshift blanket. 'Is she going to make it?' Mandy asked.

Her mum stood up. 'Let's hope so, thanks to you two!' She told them to hop into the car. 'She was pretty far gone. Mandy, you sit here. Let the dog rest her head against your knees. Talk quietly to her and keep her calm while I drive back home.'

Quickly Mandy climbed in and followed instructions.

James stood by the Land-rover, checking that Mandy and the dog were safely inside. 'I'll go back for your bike and cycle down,' he told her as he closed the door.

Mandy and Mrs Hope agreed. Emily Hope reversed into a gateway, turned and set off, roaring down the moorside. In the back of the car, Mandy softly stroked the dog's dark head, lying in her lap, staring up at her with her big, faithful brown eyes. 'Please get better,' Mandy whispered. She felt she'd never wanted anything more in her life than for this beautiful, gentle creature to return to health.

Simon ran out into the surgery yard as the Land-rover drew up. He opened the back door and gathered the patient in his arms. Adam Hope stood waiting at the door.

Stiffly Mandy clambered out, following Simon and her mother. 'I don't think there are any broken bones, just cuts and sores. She's badly dehydrated,' Mrs Hope reported. 'We need to remove something sharp from her left front pad and treat the infected area. Otherwise, it's a case of warmth, lots of liquid, and rest.' She hurried into the surgery.

Simon laid the dog on a treatment table, leaving the warm cover over her. She raised her head.

Mandy's dad took a look. He felt gently with his fingertips, checking joints, listening for the heartbeat through his stethoscope. He looked up at Mandy. 'She doesn't seem too bad,' he said. 'Very thin, though. It's a disgrace!' His voice was low and intense. 'How can people let an animal get into this condition?'

Emily Hope put on some rubber gloves and took a pair of fine tweezers from the sterile unit. She crouched down, talking gently to the dog as she took hold of the injured paw, swabbed the affected area and deftly pulled a sharp object from the wound. She held it up to the light. 'A splinter of glass,' she reported.

The dog whined and tried to rise.

'Steady,' Simon said. He stroked her neck.

'Look, she wants to get up!' Mandy said. The dog had struggled free of the jacket.

Adam Hope nodded. 'Let her try. Let's see if she can make it. She looks a determined sort.'

Simon eased the jacket away completely. They could all clearly see her starved, shaking body. Slowly she bent her back legs under her and eased herself up at the front. She straightened the back legs until at last she struggled up on to all fours.

Mandy came forward with a bowl of clean drinking water. She put it down within easy reach. Soon the dog lapped noisily, her flanks heaving, her tail wagging low and slow as she drank.

Mr Hope smiled. 'She's tough,' he said admiringly. 'I wonder where she came from.'

'Is she lost?' Mrs Hope wondered. Satisfied with the treatment, she began to clear away.

Simon folded his arms and watched the dog enjoy her drink. 'This type of dog doesn't usually get lost. Their sense of direction is too good. She's more likely to have been abandoned, I'd say.'

Mandy frowned. 'You mean, someone just dumped her?' She couldn't believe that anyone would do such a thing.

Her dad held up his hand. 'Now, we're not sure.

There may be a worried owner out there, searching high and low.'

They all stood and considered this. 'How can we find out?' Mandy noticed the dog wanting to jump down from the table, but she was too weak to attempt it. Checking first with her dad, Mandy went to help. She lifted the dog and set her gently down on the floor.

'Hmm . . .' Mr Hope stroked his beard. 'Let me ring round. Someone might have heard of a Border collie that's gone missing.'

Mandy knew that her father was in close touch with all the vets in the area. His network of friends and colleagues might well turn up with the owner. She nodded. 'Do it now, please, Dad!'

He smiled at her earnest expression. 'Right away.'

'And you could try the RSPCA and the Canine Defence League,' Emily Hope suggested. At last she found time to take off her own jacket and scarf. Her long, wavy, red hair hung free.

'Say it's an emergency,' Mandy pleaded. 'Say she's got no collar, so we haven't got a clue where she's from. Someone's probably frantic about her!'

Nodding, Mr Hope went out into reception.

Mrs Hope came up to Mandy and put an arm round her shoulder. 'Don't raise your hopes too high,' she warned.

'Yes, but . . .' Mandy began to protest.

'Look, maybe there's no frantic owner out there. Maybe the *last* thing that person wants is to get a phone call just before Christmas saying that we've found their dog. Like we were saying, the collar's missing. And these sheepdogs are bred and trained to know their way around. They hardly ever get lost.' She shook her head. 'We'll do our best. But don't expect too much, Mandy. We'll just have to wait and see.'

Mandy hung her head. She was glad when, five minutes later, they heard James come running into the surgery. It broke the anxious ticking of the clock. 'The dog's fine,' she told him, watching him crouch down and put an arm round her neck.

James stood up straight and gave a little skip of success.

'Dad's ringing round now to see if we can trace where she came from.'

They waited all evening for a return call; the news that a sheepdog had been reported missing from a farm on the other side of the county, or that a child in Leeds or York was pining over a missing pet. But the phone didn't ring. Night drew in, and Mandy and James made the dog comfortable in a warm bed in a kennel in the residential unit at the back of the surgery.

Mandy gave her a small amount of minced food. The dog came and nuzzled gratefully against her, then sank into bed. Mandy smiled softly, turned off the light and left her to sleep.

Four

Next morning, Mandy woke and looked out of her bedroom window to see a hard frost covering the ground. She ran downstairs, but before she could ask, her mother shook her head. 'No. No news,' she said. 'But we know one thing for sure; if that poor animal had stayed out last night, there's no way she would have survived! She would have died of hypothermia, and that's a fact!'

Mandy sat down to breakfast, sipping slowly at her orange juice. 'But you think she's been abandoned?' she asked.

'It's beginning to look that way.'

Mandy shook her head. It was unbelievable; the

beautiful dog was unloved, unwanted. And that left them with a problem; who would take her now?

In the middle of this puzzle, Mandy's grandparents called in. They were on their way to Walton, the nearest town, and Gran was armed with a long list of food for the party: dog biscuits, apples, carrots, sugar-lumps and birdseed. Grandad kept the human list safe in his pocket: bread-rolls, cheese, sausage-rolls, crisps, chocolate biscuits.

They came into the kitchen to see Mandy brooding over her cornflakes. 'A penny for your thoughts?' Grandad said.

Mandy gave a wan smile.

'What's wrong, love?' Gran came and sat at the table, her voice full of concern. 'I can tell the party isn't uppermost in your mind, for a start.' She put away the list that she'd intended to discuss with Mandy. 'In fact, I can see you're not yourself at all.'

Mandy let her empty spoon droop into the bowl. 'We rescued a dog yesterday,' she explained. 'It was starving to death, up on the moor.'

Gran patted her hand. 'Well done, dear. But what's the trouble?'

'She's gorgeous, Gran. Absolutely beautiful. Her face is so trusting. You just have to look into her eyes and you can't help falling in love with her!' To

Mandy, this wasn't just any old dog. She felt from the start that she'd rescued someone very special.

Gran nodded. 'So?'

'So, how can anyone bear to part with her?' Mandy felt a lump rise in her throat. She was unable to go on.

Gran got to her feet. 'Why don't you show me and Grandad this wonderful creature?' she suggested with a smile. 'I'm sure we'd love to take a look.'

Willingly Mandy obliged. She led her grandparents round the side of the house to the unit, through the door and down the row of kennels where the surgery's overnight patients stayed. A brown and black beagle sat, its head cocked to one side. A King Charles spaniel wagged its tail. At the end of the row, they came to the stray Border collie.

'Well!' Grandad bent forward and peered through the wire mesh. 'She looks happy to see you.'

Mandy unbolted the door. The dog was still too weak to jump up, but she wagged her tail. 'Come on, girl; let's take you for a little walk.'

The dog trotted obediently after her.

'She's limping,' Gran pointed out.

Mandy explained about the splinter of glass. 'The foot's already getting better, though.'

'She's very thin.' Grandad watched her limp

forward from the unit out on to the lawn. She began to sniff happily at a tree trunk, tramping through the frosty grass.

Mandy sighed. 'How could anyone do this?'

Gran and Grandad stood watching the dog. 'Do what, exactly?' Grandad had his hands in his quilted waistcoat pockets. He blew clouds of steam as he spoke.

'Dump her. Leave her to starve.'

Gran nodded. 'It's a shame. Are you sure that's what happened?'

'It looks like it.' Mandy had taken her mum's warning to heart. At first, she'd been slow to believe that the dog had been abandoned, but why had no one come forward to claim her, or put out a message to say that she'd gone missing? How had she lost her collar and name-tag, unless someone had deliberately taken it off?

The dog went and sniffed at the hedge bottom, then she trotted towards them. She sat by Mandy's side once more.

'Good girl.' Mandy bent down to pat her head.

'People do these things,' Gran said quietly. 'Especially at Christmas. They go away for the holiday. The dog's a nuisance. They can't afford to put it in kennels, so they drive into the middle of the countryside and abandon it.'

Mandy felt her stomach turn. She bent to put her arms round the dog's neck.

'They should think harder before they get a dog in the first place,' Grandad put in. 'But then, people don't. They like the look of them when they're puppies, and they buy them without stopping to consider what's involved in looking after a grown-up dog.'

'Especially at this time of year,' Gran reminded them. 'Remember, "A dog is for life, not just for Christmas",' she quoted the saying. 'Not everyone keeps that in mind, I'm afraid.'

Mandy looked up at them and sighed.

'I expect you'd love to keep her yourself?' Grandad asked. He knew Mandy's habit of caring for all waifs and strays. 'And I expect your mum and dad have had to say no?'

'I haven't asked.' Mandy knew it was out of the question; not because her mum and dad were hard-hearted, but because the house would be full to overflowing with stray donkeys, rabbits, hedgehogs, pigs, owls and lambs, not to mention dogs and cats, if Mandy had her way.

'But you'd love to find a good home for this little lady if it turns out she's been abandoned?' Grandad guessed.

Mandy nodded. 'Look at her. How could anyone turn her away?' she repeated. The dog had lifted one paw on to Mandy's knee and gazed into her face.

Gran sighed. 'You say Adam has sent out SOS messages to try to find out who owns her?'

'Yes, but no one's rung back so far. Everyone we know is passing the word around.'

'Hmm . . .' Gran stamped her feet to keep warm. She was muffled in a red woollen scarf and a red beret. 'Have you thought about taking her to Betty Hilder down at the sanctuary?' Betty ran a home for stray animals in Welford. She would be sure to find room for the sheepdog.

Mandy stood up. 'Not yet. I haven't thought that far ahead. I'd better talk to James about it first, since he helped to rescue her.'

Gran nodded. 'Betty's might be worth a try.'

Mandy turned towards the house. 'Come on, girl!' The dog stuck like glue to her side. 'I don't know, Gran. Betty would take good care of her, I know, but she doesn't have all that much space. I'd like to think of this dog getting better and running around the hillsides, like she used to. I'm sure she'd make a good working dog on a farm somewhere.' She could imagine the dog, sleek and fit, ranging across the fields, her long, bushy tail streaming in the wind.

'You're probably right,' Grandad agreed, 'judging by how obedient she is. And nice natured too.' They went into the unit and Mandy took her down to her kennel.

'Good girl,' she said as the dog went in and lay down. 'You have a rest, get your strength back.' It was probably her imagination, but she thought she could already see the dog gaining weight and recovering the gleam in her eyes, the shine on her coat. Her markings were lovely, now that she was cleaned up; black ears and eye patches with a white stripe down her muzzle, a white chest and black hindquarters.

'Can I hear the phone?' Gran asked as they emerged into the fresh air.

Mandy dashed ahead, just in time to pick up the receiver before the phone stopped ringing.

'Ah, you are there, Mandy dear!' Mrs Ponsonby's rich tones rang out. 'Do you have a moment to spare?'

'Yes, Mrs Ponsonby.' Mandy put one hand over the phone and rolled her eyes at Gran and Grandad as they followed her into the kitchen. 'Won't be a sec!' she mouthed. Then she turned back to the phone. 'How can I help? Is Pandora all right?'

'Oh, there's nothing wrong. No, Pandora's fine, thank you very much. No, this is about your little idea for a pets' Christmas party.'

'Ye-es?' Mandy waited to hear what came next. Had Mrs Ponsonby taken it upon herself to ring the vicar and get him to change his mind about the village hall?

'Well, I've been thinking. As you know, I was very much against the idea at first. I'm afraid the standard of behaviour amongst pets these days leaves much to be desired.'

'Yes.' Mandy kept her voice level. So far, Mrs Ponsonby hadn't dropped any bombshells.

'Many of them have no manners, but that's because their owners have none either, especially the young ones.'

'Is that so, Mrs Ponsonby?'

'Oh, I don't mean you, Mandy dear!' Mrs Ponsonby's singsong voice rose an octave. 'Well, anyway, I've been thinking it over. Perhaps I should let Pandora and Toby come to the party after all.'

'Great!' Mandy jumped in. 'I'm sure they'll enjoy themselves.'

Mrs Ponsonby ignored her and sailed on. 'The point is, my dear, Pandora can come and set an example to all those other badly brought up animals. She'll raise the tone of the event, if you see what I mean.'

Mandy managed not to laugh. 'I'm sure she will. And Toby too.'

'Yes. Now, my dear, since my little darlings will be able to come, I'd like to offer my own services in the organisational side of things. I'm sure your grandma already has enough on her plate, and if there's any way I could possibly help get things ready beforehand . . .'

Mandy's jaw dropped at the idea of Gran accepting help from Mrs Ponsonby. She cleared her throat. 'Actually, Gran is here now,' she said. 'Would you like to talk to her?'

Gran's eyes widened. As she came across the kitchen, Mandy dropped the phone into her hand as if it was a hot potato. Soon Gran and Mrs Ponsonby were deep into pre-party planning.

Mandy slipped towards the door. She grabbed her jacket from the back of a chair. 'I'm out of here!' she whispered to her grandad. 'I have to meet up with James. We're going to deliver more invitations.'

'Wise move,' Grandad whispered back. He nodded towards his wife, who was talking animatedly into the phone. 'I'm afraid this could take some time!'

So Mandy and James cycled around, handing out invitations and getting in the mood for Saturday's party.

That evening, Mandy sprawled on the rug in the warm kitchen at Animal Ark, one arm round the sheepdog's neck, trying to believe even now that the phone *would* ring, and a worried owner would be reunited with a faithful pet.

But no such luck. The phone stayed silent. Mandy's one comfort, as she went to bed on that Tuesday night, was that the dog was looking much better. She'd been fed and rested, brushed, pampered and made to feel special. After another good night's sleep she would be almost back to normal.

Next morning, Mandy arrived in the village just in time to see James being dropped off outside McFarlane's post office. His dad lifted his bike out of the back of their estate car, closed the door and climbed back into the driver's seat. He gave a wave and drove off in the direction of Walton, the nearest town to Welford.

'Only four days to go!' James greeted her. He took off his glasses to polish them. 'We'd better get a move on with these last invitations. How's the sheepdog?' he asked, all in one breath.

'Much better.' Mandy waited for him to mount his bike. 'She's eating like a horse.'

'Great. Hey, guess what, they've forecast snow before the weekend!' James slung one leg over the saddle.

'A white Christmas!' Mandy really liked this idea. It would add an extra something to their party.

'Just so long as it's not too deep for people to get through,' James warned. He was thinking ahead as usual. 'Where to first? Ernie's house?'

At last they were ready for another busy morning delivering cards.

Ernie Bell lived near Walter Pickard at the end of the small row of stone terraced houses by the side of the Fox and Goose. He came to the door and received his invitation straight-faced. 'Eh, I don't know about that,' he said slowly. Sammy, the grey squirrel, sat perched on his shoulder. 'Parties aren't really my cup of tea.' He rubbed his grizzled white head.

Sammy puffed out his cheeks and darted across his shoulders, chattering excitedly.

Mandy laughed. 'Sammy doesn't agree, do you, Sammy?'

'He likes parties!' James said.

The squirrel chattered back.

'Lydia will be there,' James added. 'She's bringing Houdini.'

'Is she now?' Ernie was weakening, they could see.

Just then, another grey head popped out from the far end of the terrace. It was Walter, Ernie's drinking

pal. 'He'll be there, don't worry, you young ones. I'll
see he puts on a smart collar and tie.'

James ran along to deliver Walter's own card. 'No
need for that,' he explained. 'You can make a party
hat for the competition if you like. Otherwise, come
dressed however you want.'

Walter grunted. 'We'll think about that, young
man.' He pocketed his invitation and went on
badgering Ernie to accept.

Sammy joined in, hopping up and down Ernie's
arm. 'We'll see,' he said at last.

'That means yes.' Walter winked at James. The two
old men shut their doors and James and Mandy went
on their way, across the carpark to the pub to find
John Hardy.

'Do you think he's home from boarding-school?'
Mandy asked, as they knocked at the back door
of the pub.

James nodded. 'I saw him the other day.'

When John came downstairs in his neat cream
Aran sweater, he was delighted with his invitation.
He promised to bring along both Button and Barney.
'Imogen's away for the whole holiday,' he explained.
'I'm looking after the rabbits for two weeks.' Their
arrangement to share the care of the twin brown
rabbits was working out well.

'At least you won't have far to come to the party,' Mandy told him. 'We all plan to meet up here with lanterns and torches, and we'll walk in a procession down to the village hall. Will that be OK?'

'Brilliant!' John's eyes lit up. 'Thanks for asking me!' He waved them on their way.

Next came Susan Price's invitation. They found her exercising her pony, Prince, in the frosty paddock at the back of her huge house, The Riddings. Rider and horse made a smart combination; Susan erect in her saddle, Prince beautifully groomed and healthy. Mandy could tell that Susan was genuinely pleased not to be left out of their plans. She leaned from the saddle and took her invitation. 'Party hats, eh?' she said thoughtfully. 'Well, we'll see what we can do!'

James and Mandy left her to ponder and cycled on to Greystones Farm along the valley bottom. 'Hi!' they called to Ken Hudson, at work in a nearby field. He carried food to the hardy Saddleback pigs. 'Have you seen Brandon?'

'In the barn with Ruby!' he yelled back.

They went on, and sure enough, they came across the tall, gangling figure of Brandon Gill, busy forking bales of hay on to a trailer, with round, cheeky Ruby the pig squatting on her haunches, idly watching.

Ruby turned to the barn door and spotted them,
gave a small squeal and trotted up. James bent to
scratch her pink and black back.

Mandy held out the card to Brandon. He blushed
deep red and mumbled his thanks. The envelope
was quickly shoved into the pocket of his denim
jacket.

'Can you come?' Mandy asked.

He nodded.

'Seven-thirty. Bring Ruby,' James reminded him.

'Just try and stop her!' Brandon laughed. 'You

know Ruby; she gets her nose into everything!'

Ruby grunted and snuffled at James's shoes. He took one of Blackie's dog biscuits from his pocket and held it out to the pig. Ruby snaffled it delicately from his palm with her soft, velvety snout.

And then they were off again, heading on to the main road, pausing for breath at the village crossroads. 'What about Claire?' James asked. 'I suppose she really can't bring the hedgehogs, but it would be more fun for her if she didn't have to come on her own.'

Mandy thought about it. 'It's a problem, I know.' Little Claire McKay was devoted to her prickly winter lodgers in her hedgehog refuge, but even she would realise she couldn't disturb their hibernation to bring them to a party. For a while, Mandy was as stuck as James. 'Wait, I've got an idea,' she said at last. 'That is, if you wouldn't mind . . .'

James grinned. 'Go on, Mandy. Spit it out!'

'Well, it's just a thought. Could you lend Blackie to Claire? They get on well, don't they? And that would still leave Eric for you to bring.' She knew it was a big thing to ask James to trust Claire with his dog. But at least it would give him the chance to bring along his cat.

James hardly hesitated. 'Fine!' he agreed.

'Oh, James, that's great! Why don't you go and tell Chaire? See if she thinks it's a good idea. I'll just nip over to Dorian's place and ask Andi if they can come along.'

'Meet up at your place for lunch?' James asked.

She nodded. Even though preparations for the party were in full swing, there was still a lot to do. They cycled off in different directions. As she headed for Manor Farm, Mandy hoped for great things; a grand get-together at the Fox and Goose, a Christmas card scene of snow, holly and robins, a candlelit procession up the dark street, and mountains of food!

Five

Wednesday lunch-time arrived before Mandy knew it. She hurried home after her visit to Manor Farm to meet up with James and grab a bite to eat. To her surprise, she found her dad playing with the Border collie in the warmth of the kitchen.

'I just took her out of the unit to check her over,' he explained.

But Mandy knew better; he hadn't been able to resist the dog's lovable face and trusting eyes.

'Adam, you're going soft in your old age!' Mandy's mum stood at the stove, heating a large pan of vegetable soup. She smiled as Mandy's dad rolled the dog on to her back and tickled her stomach.

'No way!' The good-natured game continued, as the dog squirmed on to her feet and bounced up with her front paws against Mr Hope's stomach. 'Ouch! No, I'm just making sure she's recovered from her ordeal,' he said.

'It looks as if she has.' Mandy nodded and laughed. 'It's great, isn't it? But have we had any word about where she came from yet?'

Mr Hope shook his head. 'A big negative on that one, I'm afraid.'

Mandy sighed. 'I wonder what she's called?' She went to stroke the dog's nose. 'It seems wrong to just think of her as "the dog" or "the stray". She must have a name that she would answer to.'

'Why not give her one?' Mrs Hope suggested. She ladled hot soup into four bowls. 'You and James. I reckon you're entitled to do that, since you were the ones who rescued her.'

Mandy nodded and felt her face glow with pleasure. She waited impatiently until James arrived, then sat with him over the soup and crusty bread. The dog snoozed in a warm corner, tired out by the game, while Mandy and James made yet another list.

'Lassie . . . Jessie . . . Badger?' James suggested.

'Patch . . . Winnie . . . Sally?' Mandy tried out

several names. None sounded quite right. They thought again.

'Flora?' Mr Hope chipped in.

They shook their heads.

'Jemima, Ermintrude, Gwendolen,' he suggested, rattling them off.

'Dad!' Mandy raised her eyebrows. 'You can't call a dog Ermintrude!'

'Gwen wouldn't sound too bad,' James added.

Mandy looked at the dog. She'd opened her eyes, head resting on her front paws, seeming to take some interest in this naming game. 'Gwen?' Mandy experimented. There was no response. 'How about Tess? Tess, here, girl!' she called softly.

The dog stood up and walked smartly towards her.

'Sit, Tess!'

She sat.

Mandy looked at the others in pleased surprise.

'Tess it is!' said Mrs Hope.

Everyone was delighted. 'Do you think that really is her name?' James asked.

Adam Hope shrugged. 'Who knows? All I can tell is she seems to like the idea.'

'Tess suits her, doesn't it?' Mandy felt it was a good name for a working dog; short, sharp and sturdy.

'Tess thinks so,' James laughed. 'You'd better watch

it, Mandy. You're already her best friend.' He watched the dog licking Mandy's hand and putting her head on her lap.

'Seriously,' Mrs Hope agreed. 'We mustn't let her get too attached. Remember, we can't keep her.' She looked kindly at Mandy before she cleaned up the lunch things.

Mandy stood with a sigh. 'Down, Tess,' she ordered. 'And we still have loads to do for the party, so I'd better get you back to the unit. There's a good dog.' Quickly she led her outside, through the yard to the residential unit. 'Good girl,' she whispered as she locked the door.

Leaving her there was hard. Try as she might to toughen up and be sensible over Tess, Mandy had to admit that the dog had touched her. In fact, she was head over heels in love with the gentle, affectionate creature.

James peered at Mandy as they pocketed the last of their invitations and set off on their bikes once more. 'Are you sure you're OK?' he asked.

She nodded. 'Yes, thanks. Where to now?' Her head was still in a whirl over Tess, and her heart wasn't in the task for the afternoon.

'The Spillers',' he suggested. They cycled in silence

towards the moor, where Jack Spiller and his family worked their smallholding. James carried an invitation for six-year-old Jenny Spiller and her pet sheep, who was also named Blackie. James seemed to be thinking long and hard. 'Mandy,' he said, 'you don't think Jack Spiller might . . . I mean, he keeps a few sheep . . . He might . . . want to take Tess!' At last he managed to get the words out, holding his breath for Mandy's reaction.

Mandy felt her heart give a little jolt at the new idea. She caught her own breath and pedalled silently along a flat stretch of road. The Spillers were nice people. They already had a working dog on the smallholding. She tried to think it through. If Tess had to go somewhere, she realised the Spillers would make good owners for her. 'Let's ask,' she agreed. It was better than Betty Hilder's sanctuary, and that was the only other idea they'd come up with so far.

As they arrived at the house, Jenny Spiller came running to meet them them, with Blackie close on her heels. He'd already grown into a sturdy young sheep.

'And everywhere that Jenny went . . .' James laughed at the sight of the inseparable pair.

Soon Jack Spiller appeared at the door. 'What

brings you two up here?' he called.

James explained about the party. Jenny jumped up and down in excitement. 'Can I go, Dad? Please!'

Jack Spiller readily agreed. 'Thanks for asking her. I'll drive her down. Half-seven on Christmas Eve, you say?'

Mandy stood by while James and Mr Spiller made the arrangements. She felt her stomach turning nervously. Finally, as the smallholder looked at his watch and took Jenny by the hand, she plucked up courage to speak.

'Mr Spiller, would you by any chance be able to take an extra dog?' she asked straight out. There seemed to be no point sidling into the issue. 'Only we've rescued a stray, and so far no one has come forward to claim her. We need to find her a good home. James thought you might be able to do with the extra help?' She gripped her handlebars tight and waited for the answer. The icy feel of cold metal seeped through her gloved hands.

Jack Spiller halted and turned. 'A working dog?'

Mandy nodded. 'A Border collie. A female. She's ever so gentle. We've called her Tess.' She found it hard to keep her voice steady, but she was determined to do her best to find the dog a good home.

'Female?' Jack Spiller slowly began to shake his head. 'That would mean we'd have two bitches round the place,' he said. 'That wouldn't work, I'm afraid. They wouldn't get on. Now if it had been a male, we might have found room for him!' He smiled at Mandy. 'It's no go, I'm afraid.'

'Thanks anyway, it was just an idea,' she said. Suddenly she realised how much she'd pinned on Mr Spiller saying yes. Tess would have loved it up here, working for her keep.

'Sorry. Better luck next time,' Jack Spiller said. He led Jenny back to the house, with Blackie trundling along behind.

Mandy sighed and looked at James. He shrugged. 'Nearly,' he said.

'So near and yet so far,' she agreed. They set off down the hill.

'Right!' James set his jaw and sounded determined. 'We're not going to let this problem ruin our Christmas, are we?'

Mandy took up the challenge. 'We are not!'

'We are going to get Tess settled in a brilliant new home before the party!' he insisted. He let go of his brakes on a straight, downhill stretch.

Mandy followed, feeling the wind in her hair. 'We are!' She began to smile as they swooped down into the valley.

We will work this one out!'

'We sure will!'

'We will not give in!' he shouted over his shoulder.

'Never!'

By the time they'd reached the bottom of the hill, Mandy had shaken off her regrets about parting with Tess. She knew they owed it to everyone to do their very best to find a home for the dog before Christmas.

Mandy's gaze swept along the road by the riverside. 'Have we got time to pop over to Greystones?' she asked suddenly.

'Of course. Why?' James was catching his breath after the downhill charge.

'Wait and see. It's my turn to have an idea!' she grinned. She cycled ahead.

'But we gave Brandon and Ruby their invites yesterday.' James gasped to keep up. They sped between bare hawthorn hedges, still white with frost. Soon the grey, square building came into view.

'I'm not looking for Brandon.' Mandy put on her brakes and squealed to a halt. She came level with the field where the Gills kept their pigs. 'I'm looking for Ken!'

Ken Hudson was the pigman at the farm. He was small and wiry, a no-nonsense sort of man who'd recently moved to live with his sister on her upland farm. He still worked here in the valley at Greystones Farm. James spied him now, crossing the field between the arched shelters where the black and white pigs lived and fed. He carried two buckets of food and whistled as he walked. 'There he is!' James pointed to him emptying the buckets into a metal trough.

Mandy spotted him too. She laid down her bike and jumped over the wall into the field. Several pigs came running towards her, including Napoleon, the huge, friendly boar. 'Hi, Ken!' She waved both arms, glad to see him put down his empty buckets and stride downhill. James joined her, and together they scratched the backs of the pigs and let them rootle around their feet.

'Now then, what can I do for you?' A smile wrinkled up Ken's thin face. He shifted Napoleon out of the way with a hefty shove, and stood with hands on hips, his cap tilted back on his head.

'Happy Christmas, Ken!' Mandy grinned. She liked Ken. His looks reminded her of a wizened jockey; skinny and bow-legged in his black wellington boots.

'Nay, you've not cycled all this way just to wish me Merry Christmas,' he countered. He looked quizzically at Mandy.

'We came to see how you got on with your move,' Mandy continued. 'Didn't we, James?'

'Yes!' He gave her a sideways look.

'It went like clockwork.' Ken scratched his forehead. 'I didn't have much stuff to shift. Got it all up to the farm in one go and settled in grand. Dora's been feeding me up since I went to live with her.'

'That's good.' Mandy shifted from one foot to the other.

'And?'

'And what?' She opened her eyes wide.

'And what else can I do for you?' Ken half-smiled. 'You can't kid me; you're up to something, Mandy Hope!' He turned to James. 'She is, isn't she?'

'Search me.' James tried to look innocent. But he gave Mandy a quick shove.

'You like dogs, don't you, Ken?' Mandy had decided the best tactic this time was to go slow and easy.

'I like everything that goes on four legs,' he

answered. Napoleon nudged against him, sniffing at his pocket. Without thinking, Ken dipped in his hand and offered the boar a wrinkled windfall apple.

'You'd like Tess, then.' Mandy gazed up at the frosty moorside, a tartan scarf knotted round her neck, her green jacket zipped tight.

'Who's Tess?' Ken filled the pause.

'Tess is a great dog, isn't she, James? Ever so friendly. And she does everything you tell her. She's a black and white Border collie with big brown eyes. I'm sure she could be a champion dog!'

'Whose dog is she, then?' Ken sounded interested.

'Ah!' Mandy held the suspense.

'I've not heard of a new dog round here,' he insisted. 'She sounds like she might be a bit special!'

'She is! Would you like to see her?' Mandy felt him grab the bait. She knew Ken wouldn't be able to resist the build-up she'd given the dog.

'Maybe.' He considered it, his head to one side.

'Why don't I bring her over?' Mandy offered.

But Ken shook his head. 'Not here. I'm heading home now, up to Dora's place. I've finished work for the day.'

'Well, we could bring her up. In fact, we'd love to. We could put her through her paces for you, if you like. She's brilliant to watch.'

'She is, is she?' Ken looked suspiciously at Mandy.
'A wonder dog?'

At last Mandy decided to come clean. 'The fact is,
she needs a new home. I thought you might take
her.' Again she held her breath.

'You did?' As usual, Ken answered with a question.
Mandy nodded.

Ken tugged at the peak of his cap. He looked down
at his boots. 'A new home?' he repeated.

'Tess is a stray. James and I rescued her. She really
is a fantastic dog, Ken! I'm sure you'd love her!'

Ken studied Mandy's eager face. 'A Border collie?
A champion?'

'I'm sure she could be! You could train Tess to do
anything. What she needs is a place where she could
be put to work rounding up sheep. You've got to
take a look at her and see!'

'Maybe there's room for another dog alongside
Whistler,' Ken admitted. 'Mind you, I don't know
what Dora would say, but . . .'

'We can bring Tess up to show you!' Mandy
couldn't contain her excitement. She ran up to Ken,
her face shining.

He nodded. 'Why not?'

James whooped and jumped up.

'Bring her up first thing tomorrow. Let's have

a look at this marvellous sheepdog,' he told Mandy. 'After all, I can't see any harm in taking a look, can you?'

Six

To the outsider, Dora Janeki's sheep farm was a miserable place, cut off by steep hills and bare expanses of brown, wintry heather. But it was sheep farm country; wild and unwalled, where sheep grazed in the distance and the dogs ran far and wide on each fetch.

Tess sat in the back of the Animal Ark Land-rover with Mandy and James at her side. Mr Hope had offered to drive them up to meet Ken Hudson early on Thursday morning, before he began his rounds. 'I'll pick you up on the way back,' he said, as he came to open the back door. Tess jumped down and sniffed the heather, her tail curving up in an elegant arc. It had a white tip that seemed to float among the low brown bushes. 'Don't expect her to do too much,' he warned them. 'She's still building up her strength, remember.'

Mandy nodded. 'Thanks, Dad. See you later.'

She and James jumped down after Tess. The weather had turned cloudy, with a strong, cold wind. It was one of those winter days when it seems it will never get fully light. Mandy pulled her tartan scarf round her chin and whistled Tess to heel.

'Good luck!' Adam Hope jumped back into the driver's seat and leaned out. 'I'll keep my fingers crossed!'

They waved him off, then turned to tramp up a bridle-path to Syke Farm. Sensing the freedom of the open spaces, alert and eager, Tess loped beside them until they reached the bare farmyard. Then James went ahead to knock at the faded red door of the house.

Mandy kept Tess back as she watched Dora Janeki come to the door. She spotted Whistler, the farm dog, peering out of his kennel at the far side of the yard. He was a tall, rangy animal, with a long grey coat. He was speckled all over with small patches of black, and his left ear was black too. His eyes were a strange pale grey colour, almost white. Now she saw his hackles rise, and he growled as he spotted Tess.

'Yes?' Mrs Janeki looked suspiciously at James. Small and skinny, like her brother, but without Ken's friendly smile, she was a short-tempered woman with sharp, poker-straight features. Mandy knew her reputation as a worrier and a skinflint, and realised now that she certainly didn't welcome visitors.

'Hello, I'm James Hunter. We've come to see Ken,' James explained.

Dora grunted. 'That's the first I've heard of it. Are you sure?' She quietened Whistler with a sharp word and frowned at the newcomers.

'He asked us to bring Tess up to see him.' Mandy put Tess on a lead and walked forward. 'He said he'd like to take a look at her.'

'Did he now?' The frown deepened. 'I can't think why. Wait here.'

She closed the door abruptly and vanished. Mandy felt her hopes dive as they stood in the cold, wintry yard.

But they revived when Ken emerged, wrapped up against the weather in a high-necked, thick, green sweater and a big blue duffle coat, wearing his cap low on his forehead. He closed the door behind him and stamped his feet. 'You're in good time,' he said, glancing at Tess. 'This is her, is it?' He began to walk round her in a slow, wide circle.

'Sit, Tess!' Mandy felt the dog stir uneasily. A few metres off, Whistler kept up his low growl. 'Stay, girl,' she said quietly, praying that Tess would submit to Ken's inspection.

Ken walked full circle, then came up to them. 'Thin as a rake,' he commented, still staring down at Tess.

'So would you be if you'd been through what Tess has just been through.' Hurriedly Mandy described the dog's long, cruel walk; how they'd found her weary, starved and footsore, on the very point of collapse. Throughout the story, Tess sat quiet, one eye on Whistler, waiting for the next command.

'She's not strong, then?' Ken bent to run his hand down Tess's long, black and white coat.

'She soon will be,' Mandy promised. 'She's getting the best treatment. We're building her up on food and vitamins. And she's tough. You'd be amazed at how quickly she was back on her feet.'

'Hmm.' Ken crouched down. The dog looked back at him curiously. 'And she'll do anything you tell her?'

'Yes. Do you want to see?'

Ken gave a brief nod.

'Stay, Tess!' Mandy gave the clear order. Then

she and James moved off across the yard. Tess sat still as a statue, with Ken looking on. 'Here, Tess!' Mandy called. Tess bounded forward and joined them in a flash.

'Let's try something else,' Ken suggested. He scouted around for a piece of broken branch from the bare horse chestnut tree which overhung the yard.

'Good girl, Tess!' Mandy breathed. She held up crossed fingers to show James.

'Brilliant,' James agreed. He patted the dog and stood up to see what the next test would be.

Ken came across with a stick. 'See if she'll fetch this when you tell her.'

Mandy took the stick and showed it to Tess. The dog sniffed and frisked up at it. Then Mandy turned away from the house and threw the stick towards the moor with all her might. 'Fetch, Tess!' she called.

And the dog was gone, streaking through the heather as the stick arched through the air. She bounded out of sight. The stick landed. Tess reappeared with it clamped between her jaws. Quickly she ran back to Mandy and dropped it at her feet. Then she sat, front paws neatly together, head up, panting, her tongue lolling out.

'Good girl.' Mandy smiled with relief. She turned to Ken.

He nodded. 'Not bad. Now let's take her up on to the moor and see how she gets on with the sheep, shall we?' He led the tramp across country towards four or five distant white specks.

James and Mandy struggled to match the tough little farmer's pace, but Tess loped easily, seeming to know exactly what was expected of her now.

'I only hope she can do this!' James whispered to Mandy. 'You don't think we're expecting too much?'

Mandy's own heart was in her mouth, as eventually they came to a stretch of short, firm grassland. The sheep were now in the near distance, a couple of hundred metres up the slope.

'Right,' Ken said. 'Step aside, you two. Let's see what she can really do.' He gave a low, short whistle. Tess pricked up her ears and glanced at Mandy. Then she trotted to Ken and sat, waiting.

Ken gave a second whistle, higher and longer. Tess leaped to her feet and ran straight as an arrow towards the group of grazing animals. He whistled again; a piercing sound which rose high at the end. Tess's track curved to the right, round the back of the sheep. Ken gave a blast of short, sharp whistles.

She circled round and round, drawing the sheep into a tight cluster.

'Wow!' James stared open-mouthed. 'She's good!'

Then Ken's call altered. The note was lower. He was calling Tess back. She hustled and darted, headed off the front sheep, slowly turning the bunch towards Ken and driving them downhill. She brought them back without faltering once.

Wild-eyed, the sheep clustered round Ken. He called Tess to heel. The sheep scrambled away, free to take up their grazing further down the hillside. Mandy and James ran up to Ken and Tess. 'Well?' they said, impatient for his verdict.

At his feet, Tess crouched low. Her sides heaved like bellows, her pink tongue lolled sideways. 'A bit too much like hard work, eh?' Ken muttered.

'Well?' Mandy couldn't restrain herself a moment longer. 'What do you think?'

Ken looked up. 'It's not so much what *I* think. It's what the boss thinks.' He gave a wry nod towards the house. 'Dora has the final say round here.'

'But what do *you* think?' Mandy insisted. She felt the wind blow from behind. Flakes of snow began to drift from the dark sky.

Ken paused. He bent to reward Tess with a firm pat against her side. 'Champion,' he confirmed.

'If it was up to me, I'd take her like a shot!'

Tess wagged her tail. Mandy grinned at James.

'What will your sister say?' James asked. 'Will she agree?'

Ken shrugged and looked down towards the house. 'Here she comes now. Why not ask her yourselves?'

They turned in surprise to see Dora Janeki striding towards them in a long blue overcoat, wearing a checked brown scarf tied firmly round her head. She didn't smile as she approached, hands in pockets, shoulders hunched. 'Can't you see it's snowing?' she complained. 'Do you want me to call out the snowploughs to get you two back home?'

Mandy swallowed. James frowned. Ken grinned. 'You watched that, didn't you?' He went down to meet her. 'I saw you looking out of the bedroom window as I was putting her through her paces. I knew you couldn't keep your nose out for long!'

Dora sniffed. 'I don't know what you mean.'

'What did you think?' Ken insisted.

'About what?'

'Oh, pull the other one, Dora!' Ken enjoyed teasing her. 'You saw Tess at work all right. Mandy and James here want to know what you made of her.'

Dora looked up at the snow clouds, she frowned

at Mandy, she told her brother off for going behind her back, she chuntered about the cost of taking on another dog. But in the end, she gave in. 'She's all right, I suppose,' she admitted grudgingly. 'Considering we don't know a thing about her.'

'*All right!*' Ken retorted. 'She's grand, she is!' Again he patted and fondled Tess.

'And you'll keep her?' Mandy could hardly believe it.

'That depends on how much you want for her,' Dora said with narrowed eyes.

'Nothing.'

'Nothing?' It was Dora's turn not to believe her ears.

'We just want you to give her a home,' Mandy assured her.

'And something useful to do,' James added.

'In that case,' Dora said, speaking in a rush before they could change their minds, 'we'll have her, thank you very much!'

'She can stay?' James and Mandy asked together.

Dora Janeki nodded once and turned on her heel. Ken Hudson slapped his thigh and grinned. Mandy grabbed James's arm and danced round in a circle. Tess jumped up and joined in.

'I won't tell you again; it's snowing!' Dora yelled

at them. 'Don't expect me to get up a rescue party!'

Ken laughed. 'Come on, she's right. We'd better get you back down.' Together they went to the farm to wait for Mr Hope. 'My sister's bark is worse than her bite,' he whispered as they walked. 'She's really taken to Tess, only she doesn't like to show it.'

Mandy nodded. They'd got what they wanted. Tess had a home. She would be out on the hillsides where she belonged. Ken was the best; he would be firm and kind, and look after her for the rest of her life. Tess would never again be found abandoned and starving.

But as she stood in the farmyard, watching the Land-rover wind its way through the flurry of snowflakes and wind, Mandy's heart felt torn in two. Yes, she wanted Tess to stay up on the wild hill with Ken Hudson. But deep inside, it hurt to leave her. As she bent to give Tess one last hug, the dog's soft, black nose nuzzled against her cheek. She put her paw on Mandy's lap and growled softly.

'Come and see her whenever you like,' Ken said quietly.

Mandy stood up with a lump in her throat, feeling the snowflakes settle and melt on her cheeks. Wondering which were tears and which was snow, she nodded quickly, turned and walked away.

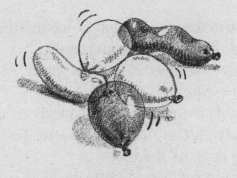

Seven

'Well done!' Adam Hope said as he stopped to pick up Mandy and James on the lonely road by Syke Farm. Tess was nowhere to be seen. Snowflakes whirled round and settled on them, then melted into glittering drops on their hair and jackets as they climbed into the warm car. 'I take it Ken said yes?'

Mandy nodded. She didn't trust herself to say anything as they set off, the Land-rover's thick, wide tyres firmly gripping the snowy surface. The wipers worked hard to keep the screen clear.

'I hope this lot doesn't set in.' Mr Hope glanced at Mandy. 'Snow may be pretty to look at and all that, but it makes a vet's job twice as difficult, and the animals don't like it much either.'

'The forecast says it'll clear later in the day,' James reported.

From the flat conversation, Mandy could tell that they too were feeling the absence of Tess's friendly face in the back of the car.

They drove on for a while in silence. Then, as Welford village came within sight and Mr Hope turned to go down their lane, he remembered a message for Mandy. 'Oh, Gran says can you two go and meet her at the village hall as soon as you get back? She wants to talk to you about decorations or something like that.'

Mandy nodded.

Her dad braked and stopped. 'Shall I drop you here to save you a walk?' He looked closely at her. 'It's best to keep busy,' he advised. 'It'll help keep your mind off Tess.'

She smiled. Her dad always had a knack of knowing what was on her mind. 'Thanks, Dad. Good idea. We'll see you later.'

'Could you ring my mum and tell her where I am, please?' James jumped out into the cold air. Already the snow seemed to be lighter, the sky clearer.

Mr Hope said he would, so together James and

Mandy jogged back into the village, heading for the hall.

When they arrived, they stamped the snow off their boots, stepped into the porch, and opened up the big oak door. Inside, Gran greeted them cheerily from halfway up a stepladder. Rolls of coloured paper streamers, glittering gold stars and packets of balloons lay scattered over the floor. Grandad was busy wedging a two-metre-high Christmas tree into a wooden barrel in the far corner of the big room, while Ernie Bell stood offering advice. 'Left a bit, now right a bit; right, right, left a bit!' he barked, until at last the tree stood perfectly straight.

'See those balloons?' Gran asked. She pointed to the packets on the floor. 'Your young lungs are stronger than ours. See how many you can blow up, while I have a go at hanging these streamers.'

Mandy and James set to work, blowing with all their might. Soon their cheeks ached and they ran out of breath. One balloon burst with a hollow bang. But the floor came alive with floating red, yellow, blue, orange and white balloons of all shapes and sizes.

Meanwhile, Gran fought the streamers. She straightened out the tangles and pinned drawing-pins into hard, wooden rafters. Then she came down the ladder and draped the streamers across the room, from corner to corner, with James's help. Grandad and Ernie were by now busy at work with tinsel and fairy-lights, decorating the beautiful tree.

At last, Mandy blew up the final balloon. James had collapsed on the floor, head propped against the wall, surrounded by a multicoloured sea of balloons.

'Let's gather them up and attach them to pieces of string,' Mandy gasped. She began to crawl on her hands and knees, chasing after them as they floated out of reach.

'That's the idea!' Gran said. 'We can hang them up around the walls.'

But just then, the outer door opened and a gust of wind whirled in and scattered the balloons. Mrs Ponsonby's voice 'whoo-hoo'ed through the hall. Grandad and Ernie cringed and carried on with their tree. Pandora came in yapping excitedly. Toby stood at the door and growled in confusion. Soon both dogs pounced into the midst of the whirling balloons.

'Hello!' Mrs Ponsonby slammed the door shut. 'Dorothy? Mandy? Is anyone there?' She peered through her steamed-up glasses, putting a pointed heel firmly through a red balloon. It popped and

the dogs ran in circles, barking loudly. 'Oh!' Mrs
Ponsonby's hand flew to her ample chest. 'Oh my!'
Pandora yapped and charged at the balloons.

'Here I am!' Gran called from the top of her
ladder. Mandy could tell she was gritting her teeth.
'What can I do for you?'

'Oh, no, no! What can *I* do for *you*?' Mrs Ponsonby
swept off her heavy tweed coat and scattered more
balloons. She flung it across the back of a wooden
chair, then rolled up her sleeves. Then she spied
Grandad and Ernie hard at work on their tree.
'Ah,' she said, 'it looks as if I arrived just in the
nick of time!' She bustled across the room. 'I always
say men have no idea how to decorate a Christmas
tree! They fling the tinsel on any old how. It has
to be *arranged*, just so!' She pushed Ernie to one
side and grabbed a piece of silver tinsel from
Grandad Hope. 'And these lights!' she said
scornfully. 'Just thrown on! Look, you have two pink
ones together and *three* blue ones! You need to
rearrange them, so!'

Ernie and Grandad Hope looked at each other
and retired, hurt. 'Let her get on with it, if she's so
keen,' Ernie grumbled. He took his cap from his
pocket and went off in a huff to the Fox and Goose.

Grandad coughed and made his excuses. 'I have

to slip down to McFarlane's for a roll of Sellotape.'
He too shuffled off.

Mrs Ponsonby nodded. 'Men!' she said. She went
on happily dismantling their tree.

While Mrs Hope stayed up her ladder, well out of
reach, and James went on chasing stray balloons,
Pandora fought on. Another balloon popped. Mandy
lay flat on the floor, chin in her hands, staring Toby
in the face. The scruffy mongrel had resigned
himself to a long wait for his mistress. He stared back
at Mandy, his mouth stretched wide in a patient, long-
suffering smile. She giggled. Balloons drifted past.
'Happy Christmas, Toby!' she laughed.

The dog lifted his head and gave one sharp bark.

'Ah, there you are, Mandy, my dear!' Mrs Ponsonby
sang out. 'Yes, and a happy Christmas to you too.
Oh, it's such a good job I came to help when I did.
How would you ever have got everything ready for
the party without me?'

By Thursday lunch-time, James had managed to
escape to his house. 'See you later,' he told Mandy.
Mrs Ponsonby was still going strong, helping to
arrange clusters of balloons along the walls. 'I told
my mum I'd be back by one. She wants me to go
Christmas shopping with her in Walton.'

'Lucky thing!' Mandy whispered back. She held up an armful of balloons to Mrs Ponsonby. 'I'll have to hang on here for a while.'

It wasn't until one-thirty that Mrs Ponsonby was finally satisfied with the decoration of the hall. Mandy, her grandmother and Mrs Ponsonby stood back to admire their work, then Gran showed them out and was able to lock the door and drive Mandy back to Animal Ark. 'Don't say a word!' she warned her granddaughter. 'If you even mention that dreadful woman's name, I shall explode like . . . Mount Vesuvius!'

Mandy sat beside her and laughed out loud. 'But the hall does look great,' she pointed out. 'It looks really Christmassy!' She felt a flutter of excitement as the day for the party approached.

'Only two days to go!' Gran said, as she stopped the car and dropped her off.

Mandy nodded and dashed into the house in high spirits. She was starving hungry, and longing to tell her mum and dad of the progress they'd made at the hall. 'The party is going to be great!' she promised. She stopped in her tracks. 'Hey, I've just remembered; I've never given you an invitation!' She stood, poised over the cups of tea she'd just poured out. 'You will be able to come, won't you?'

Her parents sat and laughed at her. 'Try and stop us!' they chorused.

Mandy gave them their tea, smiling happily.

In spite of Christmas, business went on as usual that afternoon at Animal Ark. First, Emily Hope was called out by the Canine Defence League. One of their men needed help with a dog who had been left at home alone by its owners. Neighbours had called to help the animal, but it was too distressed for one person to handle. Willingly, she volunteered to go straight across and lend a hand.

Adam Hope shook his head. 'Sometimes I think they should ban Christmas for owners like that,' he said angrily. They listened as Mrs Hope's four-wheel drive drove off.

It made Mandy think of Tess. 'I wonder how she's getting on with Ken?' she said out loud.

'Who, Tess?'

She nodded. 'I hope she settles in OK.'

'She will,' Dad assured her. 'I'd trust Ken with any animal of mine. He knows everything there is to know. And sometimes I think he prefers them to people.'

Mandy sighed. 'You're right. Can I come and help you this afternoon?' She followed him from the kitchen into the empty reception area.

'I was about to ask if you had time,' he confirmed. 'Grab a white coat. Let's help Simon clean out the residential unit before we start surgery. We've only got half an hour. Let's go!'

So Mandy went and said hello to Simon. She got stuck into her favourite work; lifting cats out of their cages and putting them gently into baskets while she cleared trays and put in food, milk and clean newspaper. Then there were dogs to exercise and groom, the floors to sweep and disinfect. They finished work with five minutes to spare before Jean was due in reception. The phone was ringing, and Mandy headed quickly back into the surgery.

She picked it up, ready to slip in an appointment or arrange visits. She hardly expected the bad news that was about to break.

'Welford 703267, Animal Ark. How can I help?' she said brightly.

'This is Dora Janeki here,' the voice snapped back. 'I need you to send someone up double-quick!'

'Yes, Mrs Janeki.' Mandy took up a pen, ready to scribble down the details.

'This is an emergency. I have a sheep here who's in a bad way. There's not a scratch on her, mind, as far as I can see. Only, something's scared her and she won't let us near. She's one of my pregnant ewes. I don't like the look of it.'

'OK.' Mandy jotted it down. 'Do you want me to send someone straight to the house?'

'No. I'll be up on the moor, waiting. She's gone down just by the wall, past High Cross. Her legs have given way, and she may not last much longer. Can you come quick?' Dora slammed down the phone.

Mandy thought quickly. She was just about to dial her mother's mobile number when she heard the car pull up in the yard. Mandy ran out and told Emily Hope the news face to face.

Mrs Hope leaned out of the window. She looked serious. 'Want to hop in?' she asked Mandy, as she revved the engine and turned the car round the way she'd just come.

Mandy jumped straight in beside her mother. They were off again, headlights glaring, speeding up the narrow roads to Dora Janeki's isolated farm.

'A pregnant ewe?' Mrs Hope swung the steeringwheel to take a sharp bend. Mandy clung on to the handhold.

'Yes. That's bad, isn't it?'

Her mum nodded. 'It can be. It depends. If the

shock's great enough, it can cause the sheep to go into premature labour.'

'So she'll have the lamb too early?'

'Yes, and that can give problems to the mother too. Internal haemorrhaging. In other words, she could bleed to death.'

Mandy gripped the handle and swung from side to side. She searched the hillside for Dora Janeki. 'There!' She spotted an old red four-wheel drive van in the distance. Mrs Hope swung her car off the road, across a rough, open track towards the van.

As she saw them approach, Dora Janeki ran across the heather to meet them.

Mrs Hope and Mandy jumped down. 'How bad is it?' Emily Hope asked.

'Come and see for yourself.' Dora shook her head. She led them twenty metres uphill to a low, crumbling stone wall. In its lee, out of the harsh wind, lay a matted grey shape. It had a swollen belly and stick-like legs. It was lying there too weak to stand.

'Can you do anything for her?' Dora turned anxiously to Mrs Hope.

'I'm not sure yet. Let's see if we can get her back on her feet for a start.'

The three of them gently tried to ease the ewe

into a standing position. But her legs buckled and her neck and head sank against the ground. They gave up and stood by to let Mrs Hope continue her work.

'It's premature labour all right.' She swiftly examined the swollen abdomen. Then she opened her bag and worked quickly to help with the delivery. Mandy watched. She could see that the sheep was already too feeble to help herself. It was with a heavy heart that she watched her mum deliver the tiny, dead lamb.

'Stillborn,' Mrs Hope murmured. 'And it doesn't look too good for the mother either.' She used a stethoscope to listen for the heartbeat. It confirmed that the sheep was suffering from heart failure and probably from internal bleeding. Soon Mrs Hope packed away her instruments and stood up. The animal lay completely still. 'I'm sorry, Dora,' she said. 'There was nothing I could do.'

Mandy stared at her mum. They stood helpless on this bleak hillside, and she felt weighed down by their failure.

Dora Janeki nodded. 'Thank you for coming. I knew we'd be lucky to save her, from the start.'

Emily Hope zipped up her bag. 'We gave it a try. What happened to her, do you know?' She was walking Dora back to her van.

'I can't say for sure. I brought Whistler up with me to drop off some winter feed. He was the one who found her. Something had terrified the poor beast. But by the time I got here, whatever it was was long gone.'

'And do you know how long she'd been there?'

'Not really. Not overnight; I know that for sure. We were up here yesterday, rounding them up, and Whistler would've spotted her then.' Dora opened the back door of her four-wheel drive and let the dog jump down. 'Wouldn't you, boy?' Dora's voice softened, then she straightened up. 'Well, that's that, I suppose.' She shook Mrs Hope's hand and arranged to send a cheque for the bill.

'I really am sorry,' Mandy's mum frowned. 'I know you could do without this just before Christmas. And it's bound to set everyone else wondering.'

Dora nodded. 'There'll be a scare now,' she admitted. 'And who can blame them? Something frightened this sheep to death, and no farmer round here will rest easy until we find out what did it!'

'I'll keep my ears open,' Mrs Hope promised.

She and Mandy watched Dora start up the engine. 'Ken will come back up with me when he gets home,' Dora said. 'He'll help me to tidy things up.' She sighed. 'Let's hope it's a one-off. We don't want any more of these in the run-up to Christmas!'

There was nothing they could say. She eased away over the farm track, leaving them to walk back to their own car.

'Well, that's that, as Dora says,' Emily Hope said sadly. She glanced once more up the hillside.

Mandy knew that her mum hated to admit defeat. 'Would it have made any difference if we'd got here sooner?'

'Who knows? But it didn't look to me as if that sheep would have survived the shock in any case. Her heart was affected. And the lamb was too little to have any chance at all. No, I don't think anything could have saved them.'

Mandy felt cold and shaky as she climbed into the car. 'But what could have done this?' she asked. 'What sort of thing could it be?'

'A dog, most probably. That's the usual thing. That's why the farmers will all be up in arms. They'll say it's a dog from the village, or even from Walton. They'll blame a townie for not keeping their dog under control. When word gets round, I wouldn't be surprised if they're all out with their guns, scouring the countryside for the culprit.'

'A dog?' Mandy found it hard to believe that a

tame pet could do this amount of damage.

'Yes.' Mrs Hope slung her bag into the back and set off down the hill. The car bumped and swayed. 'It doesn't even have to be a very big dog to worry a sheep to death.'

Mandy sighed. 'Let's hope it doesn't happen again then.'

'It's Dora Janeki I feel sorry for. She can't afford to lose livestock like this. She has a struggle to make ends meet as it is.'

Mandy sat in silence. In her mind, she saw a picture of men with shotguns, fanning out across the wintry hillside, scouring the heather and rocky outcrops for the rogue dog that had killed Dora Janeki's ewe. She went to bed that night with the image still clear. She dreamed of a dark shape hurtling at the defenceless sheep, fangs bared, springing out of nowhere. When she woke up in the morning, the telephone was ringing and she feared the worst.

Sure enough, there was another possible incident. Adam Hope had taken the call and rung off before Mandy had clambered into her dressing-gown and raced downstairs.

'That was Ken Hudson on the phone,' he reported. His face looked worried. He says a sheep from Jack Spiller's smallholding has just been brought in suffering from shock. Like before, there was no visible damage, but the poor thing was scared half to death. Jack managed to revive it by himself, and the sheep's out of danger. But the word's out. There's not a farm in the area that's not on alert.'

'But why did Ken ring you?' Mandy asked. 'If it wasn't one of their sheep?'

Mr Hope shook his head. 'Can you take some bad news, love?' He led Mandy to a chair by the kitchen table. 'Now sit down and listen to this.'

'What is it, Dad?' Mandy felt her throat go dry. She looked up into his face. 'Tell me, quick!'

'Ken rang me because in a way he's involved. Or at least, he thinks he might be, and he thought we should know.' He paused. 'The fact is, Dora has been putting two and two together. She's worked out that this sheepworrying only began yesterday when Ken agreed to keep Tess at the farm. She's come to the conclusion that the dog might not be reliable; they know nothing about where it came from or how it might have been mistreated in the past. She says a dog like Tess could easily turn.'

Mandy shook her head. She looked up in disbelief. 'Not Tess!' she said. She just knew in her heart that Tess couldn't possibly be responsible.

'No, but you can see how Dora might see it that

way,' Mr Hope pointed out. 'Ken himself doesn't know what to think. He just rang us to warn us what was going on.'

'It can't be Tess! It can't be!' Mandy would not believe it. 'Tess wouldn't do that!'

Adam Hope sighed. 'It's not me you have to convince, love!' He went slowly off to tell his wife the latest development.

'I've got to talk to Dora!' Mandy said to herself as soon as he'd gone. She jumped up. 'Dora has to understand that Tess would never do this! She has to stop spreading rumours about her!'

She ran upstairs to scramble into her clothes. She rang James and met him in the village. By nine o'clock they were on their bikes and cycling towards the farm. The mission was to save Tess from the farmers and their guns!

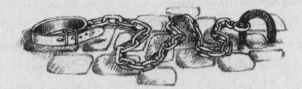

Eight

There was no sign of Dora Janeki's red four-wheel drive in the farmyard when Mandy and James arrived. Whistler's kennel was empty too.

'They must be up on the moor,' James said. 'Let's carry on up there and try to find her.'

But Mandy leaned one arm on the gate and stood to catch her breath. 'Do you think she's taken Tess with her?' She longed for a glimpse of the dog, to make sure she was still safe and well.

James looked at Mandy. 'I suppose you want to check?'

She nodded. Quickly they vaulted the steel bars of the gate and ran across the yard. 'Let's try the house first,' Mandy suggested. She went and knocked loudly at the faded door.

As they waited, they felt a cold north wind bite through their jackets. There was no reply. James shook his head. 'She must have taken both dogs.'

'Shh!' Mandy warned. She strained to listen, convinced she could hear a faint whining sound. It came, not from the house, but from the stone barn next door. She beckoned James towards the tall, windowless building. 'I think Tess might be in here!' she whispered.

James caught the sound. 'There's definitely something in there!' He pushed at the huge wooden door. It was locked. The whining grew louder.

'That's Tess. I know it is!' With a thumping heart, Mandy searched the length of the barn for a way in. Gradually the whining grew into a series of small yelps, as the dog heard their footsteps and search for another door.

'Here's one!' James had investigated the far side of the barn and found a narrow entrance; a kind of shed door. He pressed down the latch. The door swung open. 'This way, Mandy!' he called.

She ran to join him, and together they entered the dusty gloom. They heard a chain rattle on the stone floor, a dog barking out a welcome. Tess had

recognised them and strained on her metal leash to greet them.

'Tess!' Mandy ran forward and dropped to her knees. She flung both arms around the dog's neck. Tess leaned against her, furiously wagging her tail.

'At least she's still OK,' James breathed. He crouched to their level to look Tess over.

Mandy nodded. 'But they've chained her up, poor thing. Why did they have to do that?' She examined the length of heavy, rusty chain; three or four metres long, attached to the wall at one end by a sturdy ring. Mandy saw that Tess wore a new leather collar and that the other end of the chain was attached to this by a strong steel clip. Steadily she stroked the dog until Tess grew calm.

'It's not hurting her.' James tried to keep a clear head. 'I expect it's to stop the other farmers from finding her. If they knew where she was, or if they found her roaming around, who knows what they'd do to her?'

'But, look at her. Who would she attack? Poor Tess wouldn't harm a fly!' Softly Mandy stroked the gentle dog's head. Her black nose pushed against Mandy's chest and nuzzled up to her warm scarf. The white tip of her tail waved to and fro. 'It's all right, Tess,' Mandy whispered. 'Let me take this horrible thing off!' Carefully she unclipped the chain and let it drop to the floor.

Tess shook herself all over and trotted in a pleased fashion up and down the empty barn. She sniffed here and there into hidden corners. James ran to check that the door was closed.

But as he tried to push the latch down firmly, he felt someone resist from the other side. Shocked, he stepped back. He screwed his eyes against the flood of daylight as the door was flung open. A figure blocked the doorway.

'What the heck's going on here?' a voice demanded.

'Ken!' Mandy recognised him. She ran to the door. 'It's us, Mandy and James! We came to check that Tess was OK! We're sorry. We tried to ask permission, but no one came to the door.'

Ken stepped in, holding the door half-open. He kept a careful eye on Tess. 'You took her off the chain,' he said with a frown, as his eyes got used to the dark.

'Just for a few minutes!' Mandy pleaded. 'To let her stretch her legs.'

Ken nodded. 'All right then. I expect Dora's up on the moor with a vanload of food. You'd better not be here when she gets back,' he warned. 'I came back up from Greystones myself to try and calm her down over this sheep-worrying business. She's up in arms about it, I can tell you!'

'She's really mad?' James asked. He wrinkled his nose and pushed on his glasses more firmly.

Ken nodded. 'I was afraid she might do something rash, so I fed the pigs, then I came up to have a word.' His warning sent tingles of fear down Mandy's spine. 'What will she do?'

He shook his head and scratched the back of his neck. 'I don't know yet. She hasn't made up her mind. But she's fixed on Tess here as the culprit.'

Tess had gone over to James and poked her face against him. 'And once Dora has made up her mind, nothing can shift her.'

Mandy let out an exasperated cry. 'But just look at Tess, Ken! She's gentle as anything. How could anyone think she worries sheep?'

He sighed and blew the air out through his thin cheeks. 'They can fool you. They might look as if butter wouldn't melt, like Tess does now. But you turn your back for a minute, and something comes over them. They get it into their heads to go after the sheep. It's a kind of mad streak that gets into a dog.'

Mandy went and stood by James and Tess. 'But not into Tess!' she insisted. 'Dora's wrong; I know she is!'

Ken looked anxiously at the trio; Mandy, James and Tess. 'But there *is* the fact that we don't know anything about her,' he pointed out. 'She could have a whole history of being unreliable that we don't know about. Maybe that's why the last owners got rid of her.'

Mandy heard the words, but she wouldn't let them sink in. 'No!' She blocked her ears with both hands. Still Ken's muffled voice came through.

'Then there's the fact that no sheep was attacked before she came. Now we've had two in twenty-four hours. That's what makes it look bad. *And*,' he said, grinding to a decisive halt, 'the fact is, Tess went missing yesterday, when all this was going on.'

His words dropped into silence.

'Missing?' James stood up straight. 'How come?'

Ken explained. 'I wasn't here, mind. But Dora says she left Tess with food and water here in the barn, to let her get used to the place. She didn't tie her up, and she went down into the village with Whistler. When she got back, the dog was missing; probably slipped off through the side door. It was swinging open when she walked in. At any rate, Tess didn't come back till well after dark. And she looked tired out; wet and cold as if she'd been outside all that time. She just curled up in a corner and fell straight asleep. That's when Dora began to have her doubts.'

James stared at Mandy, who shook her head. it doesn't prove anything!' she protested.

'But on the other hand, it doesn't look good.' Ken put his hands in his duffle coat pockets and sighed.

'What will Dora do?' James asked.

'I don't know as yet. But I know she won't keep her on after what's happened.'

Lost for words, Mandy stared helplessly at James, then at Tess. The dog seemed to have picked up the worried mood. She sat quietly in their midst, waiting patiently.

'But what actual proof has Dora got?' James found his voice. 'Just because of the things you've said, it doesn't mean Tess is guilty!'

Ken shrugged. 'But think about it; would *you* take the risk, with what we know?'

'Yes, I would!' Mandy cried. 'Because we don't *know* anything! All Dora is doing is guessing.' She felt like crying; the success of finding the ideal home for Tess had crumbled away to nothing. Now there was even the chance that Dora Janeki would insist on having the dog put down, as a danger to livestock. Or, she might let the other, angry farmers of the district decide for her.

As they stood in silence, Tess let out a sharp, single bark. It echoed through the empty barn. She trotted up to the closed side door. She barked again.

'I think she wants to go out,' James said. 'But don't let her!'

Tess came back to them. She barked and trotted back to the door, then bounced up against the simple latch.

'Down, Tess!' Mandy ordered. The door rattled and the latch lifted slightly. Mandy went over. 'Stay down, there's a good girl.'

But Tess jumped and whirled, barking loudly. She ignored Mandy. Instead, she lunged at the latch and released it. The door swung open. Tess bounded into the open air. She turned to wait for Mandy, then ran a few steps ahead, barked and waited.

'Stop her!' James yelled. He began to run for the door.

'Stay, Tess!' Mandy put out one arm to stop James from careering ahead. 'I think she's trying to tell us something! Look, she wants us to follow!'

Tess's bark rose impatiently. She ran to the gate, stopped again, obviously meaning them to come after.

Ken emerged from the barn and shook his head. 'I don't know about this. I'm not keen,' he said.

'What is it, Tess?' Mandy ran ahead once more, sure that the dog had something important to show them. She turned in a tight, excited circle as Mandy approached, then slipped out between the metal bars of the gate. 'What is it, girl?' Mandy said, low and tense. She glanced over her shoulder at the other two. 'We have to see what she wants, at least!' she pleaded.

At last Ken gave a tight little cough and a nod. 'Fair enough,' he said.

Mandy swung open the gate and they followed Tess through.

Before long, Tess had led them clear of the farm

buildings, up towards the moor, her black shape streaking ahead. Mandy strode after her. She realised that the day was turning grey and cold. A freezing mist descended down the hillside and it was hard to keep Tess within sight. Even Ken's urgent whistle didn't stop her from forging ahead.

'Tess!' Mandy shouted, as a thicker cloud of mist seemed to swallow the dog from view. 'Why won't she do as she's told?' She turned to Ken with a feeling of panic. Tess was so set on getting them to follow that she seemed to have lost her usual obedience and common sense. 'Where are you, Tess?' she called.

They began to run up into the mist.

'Stick together,' Ken insisted. 'Whatever you do, don't split up. I don't want anyone getting lost!'

They called and ran, until they came through the billowing mist and out the other side. The view cleared, and there was Tess, sitting on a black boulder, waiting for them to catch up.

'Good girl!' Mandy cried out in relief.

Tess put up her head and sniffed the air. Suddenly, her ears pricked. She bounded from the rock and began to streak across the heather, once more ignoring Ken's expert call.

'Let's go!' James said. He began to cover the ground after her.

'Would you believe it, she's heading for those sheep!' Ken pointed to a few distant, grey specks, grazing in the shelter of a big, rocky outcrop on the horizon.

Mandy's heart sank. She knew it was no good calling Tess back now. This is what she'd wanted to show them all along; whatever it was. Mandy chased over the rough ground after James, with Ken bringing up the rear.

They ran through another band of mist, their feet crunched over narrow, iced-up streams, the wind whipped down on them. Now Tess seemed to have forgotten they were even there, racing up the hillside; a low, lean, dark shape, heading straight and fast towards the unsuspecting sheep.

'No, Tess!' Mandy gave a last, desperate call. Her heart was in her mouth. She pushed herself faster and faster, unable to believe what she was seeing with her own eyes; her beautiful, gentle Tess about to attack!

But she saw the startled sheep raise their heads and skitter sideways. They bunched together as Tess approached, looking wildly in all directions. Mandy saw Tess streak up behind them, and up the almost sheer slope on to a narrow ledge of rock. The sheep trampled into one another in their alarm, bleating loudly. One went down on its front knees and skidded several metres down the hill. The others scattered for the protection of boulders, bushes; any cover they could find.

Tess towered above them on the rock. She snarled, teeth bared.

'No!' Mandy came nearer still; a hundred metres away, begging Tess to hold back.

Tess leapt. She was on the ground, amongst the heather and the sheep, charging through them. Mandy heard a ferocious growling and snapping, bodies hurtling through bushes. She saw a sheep's terrified eyes.

Then a sharp shot rang out. Everything froze. A mist billowed across the scene, and Dora Janeki emerged, a shotgun raised to her shoulder. Whistler crouched at her heel.

Mandy caught a glimpse of Tess, lying low, but ears up, poised ready for more action.

She ran towards the woman farmer. 'Oh, don't!' she pleaded.

Then the hillside seemed to come alive with men running. Two or three followed Dora's small, stern figure, shotguns at the ready. Mandy recognised Jack Spiller and Dennis Saville, the foreman at Sam Western's farm. From lower down the hill, James and Ken ran to the spot where Mandy faced Dora. Meanwhile, the frightened sheep had scattered in all directions, and both Whistler and Tess lay quiet, warily eyeing the scene.

Dora stormed at her brother. 'What did I say?' she shouted. 'You saw that with you own eyes! I knew it was that dratted dog right from the start!' She waved the barrel of her gun at Tess. 'But you wouldn't listen!' she accused. 'And I was soft enough to hang back from doing what I knew I should do in the first place! More fool me!'

Ken sighed and shook his head at Mandy. 'What can I do?' he muttered. 'You saw it, as clear as daylight. There's the proof you were on about!'

With the sound of the gun, Mandy had felt something snap inside her. She'd believed in Tess. Yet she'd seen her leap, teeth bared, from the rock into the midst of the sheep. The shot had rung out. It was like a nightmare. With tears in her eyes, cold and trembling, Mandy gazed silently at James.

Dora pushed them to one side and strode past, heading for Tess. Jack Spiller and Dennis Saville went to back her up. They raised their guns.

'Oh, no!' Mandy put her hands to her face.

James gripped her wrist. 'Look, Mandy!' He pulled her hands away.

Tess had spotted the three shapes coming menacingly towards her. She sprang to her feet and turned. Then she was off, darting up the hill into the shadow of the rocks. Three shots rang out. Still Tess fled. She vanished behind the rocks. Moments later, they saw her again, making her way along the ridge. The farmers raised their guns.

Tess paused for a second, turned her head towards them and gave a low whine. Then, with a whisk of her white-tipped tail, she vanished out of sight.

Nine

All day Friday a light snow fell. By evening, Welford lay under a crisp white covering that sparkled in the clear moonlight. Gritting lorries came out to clear the roads, but the fields and hillsides lay under seven or eight centimetres of even snow.

Mandy felt numb. She'd seen Tess attack the sheep with her own eyes, and she knew that Dora Janeki, Jack Spiller and Dennis Saville would still be out on the snowy moorside with their guns. But she and James had taken themselves off home before the snow set in, too disappointed to talk.

Ken had rung Animal Ark to tell Adam Hope what had happened. Mandy's mum and dad came out to meet them. Gran and Grandad rallied round. They took James back to his house and persuaded Mandy to come shopping for last-minute party food. Mandy spent the afternoon and evening at Lilac Cottage, baking cakes and pastries ready for the party next day.

Christmas Eve dawned bright and clear. At eight o'clock Mandy opened her bedroom curtains to a pale blue sky and a sweep of white hillsides. The bare trees were coated in thick frost, the walls and roofs sparkled in the sunlight.

'It's a lovely day!' Emily Hope called upstairs. 'Breakfast's ready!'

Mandy pulled on some jeans and a thick blue sweater, then went down for her winter breakfast of porridge, honey and milk.

'It looks good for the party tonight.' Mrs Hope brought a pot of tea to the table. 'As long as it stays clear, there won't be any problem about getting there.'

Mandy nodded. She knew there were still dozens of things to do.

'How do you feel?' Her mum put a warm hand over hers. 'Do you think you'll be able to cope?' She pushed a stray strand of hair back from Mandy's face and gave her cheek a light kiss.

Mandy took a deep breath. 'I'll be OK, Mum. I keep thinking of Tess, that's all.'

'I know. You must be very upset.'

'I never thought for a second she would do what I saw her do. In fact, I still can't believe it.' Mandy shook her head. 'I thought I knew her!'

'It's hard,' Mrs Hope agreed. 'But I think the party will help keep your mind off things, don't you?'

'Oh, yes. I don't want to let anybody down.' Mandy finished her breakfast and got up from the table. 'Everyone's looking forward to it. The hall's all ready, except for last-minute things. I have to call in at Simon's to help him bring the music system across and set it up. Then Gran and Mrs Ponsonby will start bringing the food. In fact, I'd better get going!' She reached for her jacket and scarf.

'Good for you!' Mrs Hope smiled at her. 'We've got a busy day in the surgery ourselves. See you later.'

Mandy and her mum went their separate ways. Soon Mandy had met up with Simon and they were driving to the village hall in his battered white van, with the music system safely stacked in the back. They lifted it out and carried it through the open door, to find Grandad and Ernie already putting up trestle-tables, and Gran and Mrs Ponsonby standing by with piles of white tablecloths.

'My!' Simon put down the turntable and took a look round. He saw the tree lights winking, the balloons and the streamers. 'This should get us all into the Christmas mood all right!'

He plugged in wires and arranged speakers, then went off to work. James and Mr Hunter arrived with armloads of holly from a tree in their back garden. 'Dad thought this would look nice along the windowsills.' James peered out from behind a mountain of shiny green leaves and red berries.

Mrs Ponsonby swooped down on him and took the holly. 'Perfect!' she cried. 'I'll *arrange* them, just so!' She began to place the twigs and to order Mr Hunter around. 'Put those down there, would you? And the rest on that empty table, out of reach. We wouldn't want Pandora to hurt herself on those nasty prickles, now would we?'

Pandora snuffled up to Mandy, who picked her up and petted her. Then she set to work, helping her gran to cover the tables with clean white cloths.

During the early part of the morning other visitors dropped by. Susan Price called with boxes of Christmas crackers which her mum had sent across. 'She says there should be enough for everyone!' Susan piled the gold and silver treats into the middle of a table. 'There are party hats inside for those people who don't bother to make one for the competition.'

James stopped in his tracks. He put down a pile of plates with a clatter. 'Uh-oh, the competition!' He suddenly remembered.

'Yes, I've already made a hat for Prince,' Susan told him. 'But I'm keeping it a secret.'

James turned to Mandy. 'I've just thought of something; we haven't got anyone to judge it yet!'

'Shh!' Mandy nudged him. But it was too late.

'What's that I hear?' Mrs Ponsonby cried. 'You need someone to judge the party-hat competition? Why, I'd be glad to do it for you!' She climbed down from a chair with an armful of holly. 'No need to worry about that, my dear. Let me take one more thing off your mind. Leave it to me. I'll *organise* your little competition. In fact, let me donate the prize!'

Mandy graciously accepted the offer. 'I planned to ask Gran to be the judge,' she whispered to James with a grin.

'Oops, too late now!' He picked up the plates and began to set them out on the tables.

As Susan went out, John Hardy came in. 'My dad wondered if you could make use of these,' he said to Mandy. He carried a giant cardboard box full of packets of crisps. 'And there's a box of peanuts to follow.' For half an hour he trooped across the street from the Fox and Goose with boxes of nibbles and cans of soft drinks.

Claire McKay came next. She brought Blackie, James's Labrador dog, to see what was going on. She peeped round the door, her dark fringe framing her face, her brown eyes staring in delight at the preparations. Blackie ran ahead, wagging his tail at James.

'Hi, Claire!' Mandy called. 'Do you want to give me a hand with these paper napkins? We have to fold them up into little hat-shaped things, so they stand up, *just so*!' She grinned at James as she imitated Mrs Ponsonby, who had just popped out with Pandora and Toby on their 'walkies'.

Claire nodded and came in. She soon learned how to fold the napkins. Grandad and Ernie finished setting up tables. Gran was happy with their positions. 'Coffee, everybody?' she asked. She took a huge Thermos flask from her shopping basket, then plastic beakers and home-made ginger biscuits. 'Elevenses at half past ten!' she smiled. 'It's time for a break!'

It was only now that she had time to think that Mandy's mind swung back to sad thoughts. As she munched her biscuit, she pictured Tess, cold and miserable, cowering behind rocks, leaving telltale footprints in the new snow. Dora Janeki would be up there too, tracking her down. She imagined a final scene; Tess shivering, her brown eyes staring down the barrel of a farmer's gun . . .

Mandy broke out of the circle of chattering helpers. She reached for her jacket.

'Where are you off to, love?' Grandad asked.

'Can you manage without me for an hour or so?' she asked. 'There's something I'd like to do.'

Grandad looked at Gran. They nodded. 'Of course we can. We'll carry on here until you get back,' he said.

'I'll come!' James jumped up. He must have guessed what was on her mind.

Mandy nodded. She heard him follow her out of the hall. 'I'm going on to the moor,' she told him quietly.

He nodded. 'That's why I said I'd come.' He joined her in the yard. 'We'll have to walk.'

'Or run.' They set off at a jog up the village street. 'We might not be able to save Tess,' Mandy explained. 'Not if the farmers have their way. But there's no need for her to suffer and die that way, not if we get to her first.'

James kept pace with her. They'd cut across fields, out of the village. On the horizon, the black Celtic cross landmark showed up sharp and clear. 'What are we going to do?' he asked.

Mandy ran on with her head down. Their feet crunched over untrodden snow, sinking through the frozen crust into a powdery layer below. 'We're going to find her and take her back to Animal Ark before the farmers get her,' she promised.

'Then what?'

Mandy stopped to stare up the hillside. 'If Tess has to die because of the sheep, I'll ask my mum and dad to do it,' she said. 'If she's not going to be allowed to live any more, we'll put her to sleep at Animal Ark!'

She wouldn't let Tess feel the pain of the gunshot. She wouldn't let her end her days as a hated, hunted fugitive.

They reached the tall hedges of Upper Welford Hall and had to pause again for breath. Running uphill through soft snow was hard work. They stood gasping, as Sam Western's dogs barked out a warning. Then they ran on, past High Cross Farm, along the ridge of moorland where Dora Janeki's sheep usually grazed. Today it was empty; a white wonderland.

'She must have rounded them up and taken them into the barn.' James gazed all round. There was no sign of life.

'Because of the snow,' Mandy agreed. 'But Tess is still out here somewhere. Come on!' She forged ahead, through drifts of snow that had collected in hollows, searching for a dog's prints, heading for the wild rocks and moors.

'She could have frozen to death by now!' James pulled his own legs clear of a drift. He scanned the landscape.

'No!' Mandy refused to believe it. They plunged on, knee-deep in snow.

Way up in the hills, beyond Syke Farm, they stopped to look down on the scattered houses. So far they'd found no sign of Tess. But now James and Mandy thought they spotted a small group of people tramping across fields with a dog, each armed with a shotgun. It was too far away to see clearly, but they knew what it meant. The farmers' search for the rogue dog was still on.

'This way!' James dodged behind some rocks, out of sight. Mandy followed. They slid down a flat slope, over the ridge and down the far side.

Here the snow was less deep. There was a blown scattering of powdery flakes. A strong wind had swept the hillside clean. Some sheep remained, in the shelter of high rocks, still nibbling at patches of exposed grass. In this new valley, the sun had partly melted the snow, and crept up the frozen slopes towards the sheep. Mandy and James slid to a halt, still deep in shadow, trying not to disturb the nervous animals.

But something else seemed to attract the sheep's attention; a sound or a smell. They glanced along the hillside, then bent to nibble the grass. Mandy held James's arm. 'Wait a moment,' she whispered.

She'd spotted a dark shape crouching low behind a far rock. It was about twenty metres from the sheep, downwind of them and creeping nearer.

Mandy longed to spring up and wave her arms in warning. She wanted to get the sheep away from the prowler. But something kept her fixed to the spot. She and James crouched and stared. The shadowy shape was a dog, and every second it crept closer to the sheep.

Nearer and nearer. The dog's back was black. Its ears and nose were pointed. It had a strong, bushy tail. But the tip wasn't white. And they could see that the belly of the dog, as it crept forward, was tan-coloured. It bared its teeth, ready to pounce.

'That's not Tess!' James whispered. 'It's too big!'

'It's Major!' Mandy said, her eyes wide with surprise. 'It's the new dog at Upper Welford Hall!'

The German shepherd dog froze in its crouching position, waiting for a sheep to break from the group before he sprang.

But before anyone had time to move, Mandy felt another shape hurtle past from behind. A thin, black dog curved across the hillside between Major and the sheep, working them into a tight circle. They left off grazing and shuffled into a tight knot. The new dog hustled them and moved them off, darting at strays, rounding them up and out of danger.

'Tess!' Mandy leapt to her feet. 'She's protecting the sheep! She's trying to save them from Major!'

The rogue dog, bared his teeth and snarled. He advanced on Tess from behind.

Then James ran towards the sheep, shooing them downhill towards the sunlit valley. Once on the move they ran quickly, alert and well out of reach of their attacker.

'Tess, watch out!' Mandy warned. She saw that the Border collie was in danger herself now. Major snarled again and charged at her. Tess turned to defend herself.

Major leapt at Tess. The two bodies crashed and hurtled together. They rolled down the hillside,

before Tess twisted free. Mandy ran at them, shouting
Tess's name. Major attacked a second time. There
was a yelp, more snarls and growls. 'Major, get back!'
she cried. Mandy stood by, helpless, as Tess struggled
to defend herself.

At last the terrifying fight came to an end. Tess
broke free of Major's snapping jaws, whirled on the
spot and raced away. The other dog snapped at
nothing and backed off as Mandy and James moved
in. A deep growl rattled in his throat. He crouched
low. Then he turned tail, away from the sheep,
sloping off along the side of the valley.

'Tess!' Mandy turned back up the hillside in time to see the Border collie reach the ridge and pause. 'Here!'

But Tess had looked down the barrel of a gun and she trusted no one now. She gave a quick, sharp bark, held her head high and panted for breath. Mandy thought she met her gaze, and Tess's dark brown eyes told her that she was innocent after all.

Then she ran on out of sight, into snowy Welford valley, back towards the farmers with their guns.

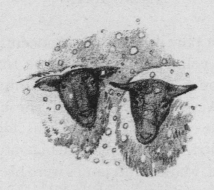

Ten

Mandy knew they had to act quickly. She ran on to the crest of the hill, too late to spot where Tess had gone. But she saw her track, running along the ridge, up the valley into the wild moorland countryside.

James grinned as he scrambled up the slope behind her. 'It isn't Tess!' he shouted. 'It's a different dog!' He dipped his hands into the snow and scooped it into the air.

'She was trying to *save* the sheep! Yesterday, when we saw her in the mist and it looked like she was attacking them, she was really fighting Major, trying to keep him off. She was *protecting* them!' Mandy joined in James's celebration. 'Isn't she brilliant?

And the best part is that she's innocent!'

She went yelling down the slope towards Sam Western's house, half-sliding, half-running. 'We have to tell Mr Western about Major!' she cried. 'He'll have to let the others know that it's his dog, not Tess!'

By the time they arrived at the big gates of Upper Welford Hall, Mandy and James were breathless and covered in snow. Two sturdy bulldogs came barking through the grounds towards them. A side door was flung open and Sam Western strode out.

He was dressed in a Fair Isle sweater and brown trousers, his greying hair combed neatly to one side. He came like a true lord of the manor down his snow-covered drive.

The two bulldogs leaped at the gate, snarls on their squat faces. Mandy and James stepped back.

'What's going on?' Mr Western looked down his nose at them. 'Oh, it's you,' he said coldly. 'The vets' girl, isn't it?'

Mandy nodded. 'And this is James. James Hunter.'

'What do you want?' Mr Western ordered the bulldogs to be quiet. 'This isn't some Christmas prank, is it?' He seemed annoyed at the disturbance.

'Oh, no!' Mandy wanted to make everything clear all at once. But how did you tell someone that his dog was a sheep-killer? She hesitated.

'I hope you're not carol singers. Because I don't pay carol singers, so you can pack up and be off,' he warned.

'No, Mr Western. It's about your dog, Major.'

A deeper frown set in. 'What about Major?'

'First of all, do you know where he is right now?' James asked. He looked round the grounds, past the frozen ornamental pond, across the lawns towards the fine old house. There was no sign anywhere of the German shepherd dog.

Western grunted. 'If you must know, he's out with my farm manager.' He raised one eyebrow, ready to send them packing. 'Not that it's any of your business.'

'But it is!' Mandy protested. 'Major must have broken free from Mr Saville. We've just spotted him over the ridge in the next valley.'

Western was caught off guard. 'Dratted dog,' he muttered. 'Why didn't you get hold of him and bring him down with you?'

'We couldn't.' Mandy looked to James again for help.

'He was attacking the sheep, Mr Western!' James came straight out with it.

The farmer let out a hard little laugh. 'Nonsense!' he began. Then he paused. 'Look, I know there's a sheep worrier on the loose,' he admitted. 'Dora Janeki told Dennis all about it. As a matter of fact, he's out there now, helping to track it down.'

Mandy and James watched Mr Western grow red in the face. They saw a puzzled look develop.

'Major went with him, as it happens. But Major's not the villain. That's ridiculous!' He tried to bluster his way through.

Mandy looked him straight in the eye. 'Where was Major on Thursday when the first sheep were attacked?'

There was a long pause. 'Now, look!' Sam Western shot her an angry glance.

Mandy stood firm. 'Where was he, Mr Western?'

'Well, he did go missing for part of that day,' he admitted. 'Dennis had to go out and round him up at about teatime. But that doesn't prove anything!' He lifted his chin defiantly.

Mandy and James waited for a few moments. The two bulldogs had calmed down and began to tramp through the snow, snapping up mouthfuls and sniffing in the hedge-bottom. 'But Major's on the loose again now,' James said calmly. 'And we've just seen some sheep being attacked. Don't you think you'd better come and check?'

Mr Western looked sternly through the bars of the

iron gates. 'Wait here!' he ordered. He called to the dogs and strode off up the drive. He disappeared through the side door and closed it with a slam. Five minutes later he reappeared, dressed in green wellingtons and a waxed jacket. His collar was turned up, and he wore a tweed hat with a curled brim, pulled well down. In one hand he carried a mobile phone, which he stuffed into his pocket.

'We'll have to be quick,' Mandy said, as he came out through the gate. 'The sooner we find Mr Saville and ask him about Major, the better.'

The three of them set off together along the track past High Cross Farm. They cut through a small hawthorn wood at the back of the empty goat field. Mandy caught a glimpse of Lydia Fawcett emerging from her barn. 'Lydia, have you seen Mr Saville?' She cupped her hands to her mouth and yelled.

'Heading up to Syke Farm!' Lydia called back.

'Thanks!' Mandy waved.

Sam Western frowned and strode ahead. 'I hope this doesn't turn out to be one of your tricks,' he muttered. 'You'd better be telling me the absolute truth, or else!'

'We are,' James promised. 'You have to talk to Mr Saville and stop him shooting the wrong dog.'

Western glanced sideways. 'The wrong dog?' he

repeated. He swung up to the right, heading for Dora Janeki's bleak farm.

'Tess,' Mandy explained. 'She's the stray Border collie we found. Dora took her in. But now she thinks Tess is the sheep-worrier.'

Western grimaced. 'And you two say it's *my* dog, is that it?' He stopped.

Mandy's heart missed a beat. 'We *saw* Major attacking the sheep, Mr Western! It was Tess who tried to save them!'

'Hmm.' Sam Western seemed to be thinking of his warm fireside and slippers. He glanced back towards his house. 'You could be trying to shift the blame here. I wouldn't put it past you.'

'No, honestly!'

He sniffed. 'Better not risk it, I suppose.' Reluctantly he trudged on through the snow. 'Isn't that Dora Janeki right over there?' He pointed to the moor, where three tiny figures were coming down the slope towards them. He raised a hand and gave a loud shout.

While Sam Western rested and waited by a low wall, Mandy and James jumped over it and ran to meet the group. They recognised Whistler by his grey mottled coat and stooped to give him a welcoming pat. 'Good boy,' Mandy breathed. She looked up to see Dora, Dennis Saville and another lad from Sam Western's farm approaching.

'It's the boss,' the lad said to Dennis. He hung back to let the estate manager deal with what looked like trouble.

Dora came down frowning at Mandy. 'We just spotted that stray dog and took a couple of shots at it. We've not struck lucky so far, but we will before the day's out!'

'But it's not Tess's fault,' Mandy began. She felt James hold her back.

'Mandy, come over here!' He drew her away to listen to the conversation between Dennis Saville and Mr Western.

'Where's the dog?' The farmer didn't bother with explanations. 'Come on, Dennis, where's the dratted thing got to?'

Dennis shuffled his feet. 'Didn't he come back to the Hall?'

Western glowered but said nothing.

'He cut back home just after I brought him out. I saw him skirting back through the side gate. I took it he was headed straight home.' Dennis Saville stood with his gun slung through the crook of his elbow. 'Didn't he?'

'He did not.' Sam Western sighed and took the

phone from his pocket. 'Let me ring and check that he's not turned up there now.' He pushed buttons to dial the number.

'What's all this about?' Dora demanded. 'Whatever it is, we'd better sort it out and get a move on. Have you seen those big, dark clouds? I don't like the look of them.'

On the horizon, a bank of heavy snow clouds gathered. The sun had sunk behind them, leaving a golden rim of bright light.

Sam Western spoke down the phone. 'What's that? No sign of Major, eh?' He listened. His frown deepened further. 'Say that again!' he demanded.

Mandy and James held their breaths. The stamped their feet and looked worried. Sam Western seemed to have gone pale as he clicked a button and put the phone back in his pocket.

'Well?' Dora was anxious to press on.

'That was a message from my secretary,' he said quietly. 'She's just had a phone call from Spillers' place. Word's going round that another sheep has been attacked, about half an hour ago. Jack Spiller's on the scene right now. No one actually saw what happened, but the sheep's in a bad way. She's losing blood. They've just sent for the vet from Animal Ark. Spiller wants the dog caught before it does any more damage. Every farmer this side of Walton is out after it!'

'See!' Mandy cried. 'You have to believe us! Major is a menace to every sheep around. Not Tess; Major!'

Her pleas fell on deaf ears.

'What's it matter which one it is?' Dora said. 'We know there are two dogs on the loose up there. And there are more sheep being savaged. Let's go!' She marched across the hill, followed by Sam Western, Dennis Saville and young Dean, Western's farmhand.

Mandy wanted to cry out in protest. Instead she turned to James. 'Why won't they believe us?'

'Because they're not thinking straight, that's why. So, *we*'ll have to. Listen, Mandy; Mr Western said that Jack Spiller rang Animal Ark. Someone will be on their way right this minute. Let's run down to the road and try to head them off. That way, we'll get to Spillers' first and explain about Major. There's a better chance that your mum or dad can make people believe what's happening than we can!'

Mandy agreed. Without another moment's hesitation, they sped off in the opposite direction to the gang with the guns, downhill towards the winding road, scanning the valley for a glimpse of the Animal Ark Land-rover.

'There!' Mandy cried. There was a gleam of windscreen lower down the valley, the faint sound of an engine, before a blast of wind drowned it and a flurry of snowflakes began to fall. They ran on towards the road.

When the Land-rover climbed into view again, Mandy and James stood in the midst of a sudden blizzard. They waved their arms and shouted. Mr Hope skidded to a halt.

'Mandy! James!' He flung open the passenger door and told them to get in quick.

'Are you going up to the Spillers'?' Mandy sank back against the seat, with James beside her.

Mr Hope revved the engine. He turned the headlights full on. 'Yes, if we make it,' he warned. 'How did you know?'

Mandy explained in a rush how Mr Western and his dog, Major, were suddenly involved; how it was Major who had attacked Jack Spiller's sheep. 'We have to stop the farmers from going after Tess!' she pleaded. 'Can you tell them that she isn't to blame?'

Adam Hope frowned and nodded. 'I'll do my best.' The Land-rover edged forward up the slippery hill. 'But remember, my most important job is to save Jack Spiller's sheep!'

Mandy nodded and hung on, as the car skidded and bumped along.

At last they arrived at the smallholding. Snow still fell thick and fast. Mrs Spiller came out to the gate and directed them off the road, along a rough track between two stone walls, already hidden by snowdrifts. 'You'll have to drive about three hundred metres up the tractor track!' she yelled. 'Jack's stayed up there with the sheep!'

They drove on. The car lurched and swayed. Soon they spotted a dark figure bending over the injured sheep. Mr Hope stopped the car and ran across, knee-deep in snow. Mandy and James ran to help.

Jack had covered the sheep with a piece of sacking to keep off the worst of the snow. There was a wound, low down on its neck, and a stain of blood on the white ground. Mandy winced as her father went down on to his knees, opened up the bag she gave him and injected the shoulder with a shot of anaesthetic. He waited for it to take effect while he cleaned the wound. 'It doesn't look as if she's lost too much blood,' he assured the smallholder. 'And at least this one isn't pregnant.'

Jack Spiller nodded. 'Are you going to put in a couple of stitches to stop the bleeding?'

Adam Hope worked fast. 'That's what I'm doing

now. There. Now, Jack, you'll have to help me lift her into the back of the Land-rover. That's right.'

Mandy and James picked up the sacking and walked behind her dad, Jack Spiller and the sheep. She handed her father his bag as he climbed up into his seat.

'Hop in the back with the patient,' he told them.

But Jack interrupted. 'There's more bad news, I'm afraid. Dennis Saville came down this way with a lad and a dog, just before you showed up. He asked me to tell you there's another one up the hill, not far off.' His face looked drawn and worried as he pointed across the snowswept hillside.

'Another injured sheep?' Mr Hope roared the engine into life, grabbed his bag and jumped to the ground again. 'Has this dog gone crazy?' He pulled Jack Spiller towards the car. 'Here, Jack; you'll have to drive your sheep down to the house in the Land-rover. Mandy and James, you stay with him. I'll have to go and take a look!'

Mandy began to protest as Jack Spiller climbed into the driving seat.

'No, get the sheep down into the warm as quick as you can!' Mr Hope ordered. He zipped his jacket to the chin, ready to set off across country.

'Dad!' Mandy said. 'Wait for me. I want to come!'

But her dad insisted. 'Stay in the car, Mandy. That's right. You'll have to help Jack at the other end. Carry the sheep inside with him. Keep her warm. Now go on, I won't be long!'

Mandy and James did as they were told. The snow gusted against the car, the wipers whined, the engine stuttered.

'Let's go,' Jack Spiller said. 'If we're not quick, the poor thing will die of cold!'

So Mandy and James clung to the bar as the Landrover rattled back down to the cottage. The last Mandy saw of her father was a small, dim figure heading into the blizzard to save another life.

Eleven

The snow fell fast and furious. At Jack Spiller's house, Mandy and James helped to carry the injured sheep into the small barn, where they settled her into a bed of straw and left Jenny and Maggie Spiller to take care of her.

'Sam Western's waiting in the house,' Mrs Spiller said. 'He wants to have a word with you, Jack.'

They went ahead and found the small kitchen swarming with people who had taken refuge from the sudden storm. Dora Janeki sat at the table with Dennis Saville and Dean. They huddled over cups of tea, guns resting against a nearby wall. Everyone avoided meeting Mandy and James's eye as they came in. Dennis shuffled his feet in embarrassment.

Mr Western himself stood by the window, clearing his throat. He took a step forward. 'Er, Jack, I need to have a quiet word.' He looked uncomfortable as he beckoned Jack across.

Mandy glanced at James. Mr Western was not his usual confident self. She listened hard, trying to overhear the conversation.

'Dennis saw it all . . . yes, the second sheep . . . he was there . . . I'm afraid it was . . . yes, Major, my new dog . . . most awfully sorry!' Sam Western muttered.

Mandy caught disjointed phrases. She held her breath as she saw Jack Spiller frown and nod. Then she couldn't bear to be in the dark any longer. She went up to Dennis Saville. 'What happened?' she asked.

'Well, we caught Major in the act,' he confessed, glancing at Dora's stern face. 'We came along the ridge looking for the Border collie, and found Major setting about another of Jack's sheep. Dean here managed to grab him from behind and we brought him straight down. We put him in the shed outside until the snow stops and we decide what to do with him.'

Mandy's eyes filled up with relief. At last they knew

the truth. She turned to Dora. 'Does that mean that you won't go after Tess any more?'

Dora nodded. 'I owe you and James an apology,' she said quietly. 'I was a bit hasty, I'm sorry.'

James came up with a smile. 'What will happen to Major now?' He stood next to Mandy in a pool of melting snow.

'That depends.' Dennis Saville kept one eye on his boss, still deep in conversation with Jack Spiller. 'We want to hear what Jack has to say. After all, it's his sheep and Betty's here that have been attacked. I think Mr Western still wants to keep him on and have him properly trained as a guard dog.'

Mandy agreed that this was a good idea. 'There's no need to have him put down, is there?' Even though Major was the one who had caused all the trouble, she would never want to see a healthy animal put to death. 'If he's treated well, I'm sure he'll improve!' She kept her fingers crossed for the poor dog, who didn't know how to use his freedom on the hillsides, after a life cooped up in a city yard.

At last Jack and Mr Western came to an agreement. 'I'll pay your vets' fees, and Mrs Janeki's too,' Western announced. 'I'll cover all the expenses that this spot of bother has caused. And I promise to keep Major well under control in future. He's a fine animal really, and I intend to look after him well.'

Jack nodded. 'If you stick to your promise and there's no more trouble from Major, I think we'd all agree with that.'

Dora Janeki too came round. She sniffed and grumbled for a while, but in the end she didn't object. It ended in handshakes, relief and smiles.

But outside the snow still fell. It whirled through the door in a great gust, as Maggie Spiller and Jenny came in to report that the injured sheep was recovering well in the barn.

'Is Dad back yet?' Mandy asked. Through the window she could see the snow drifting up to a metre deep against the farmyard walls. It was more than half an hour since Adam Hope had set off after the second injured animal.

'No. I thought he might be in here.' Mrs Spiller looked anxiously round the room. 'Shouldn't he be back by now?'

Mandy peered again through the window. She could hardly see beyond the tiny yard; the hillside was lost in the snowstorm. Dark clouds swept down, the wind gusted. There was no sign at all of her brave dad.

'Dennis, you know the spot where the sheep was.' Mr Western took charge. 'How far is it from here?'

'About half a mile. I couldn't be sure exactly. We were busy keeping Major under control.' Dennis Saville looked at his watch. 'Let's give him about ten more minutes before we start to worry.'

They agreed. The minutes dragged by. Mandy sat with her face at the window staring out, praying for the snow to ease. And still Mr Hope didn't show up.

'Right!' Mr Western broke the edgy silence. 'Let's make up a search-party. We can't wait any longer. This is an emergency.'

Mandy felt a jolt of fear pass through her. She watched the others put on their boots again and zip up their jackets. 'Can I ring my mum?' she asked Mrs Spiller.

'Of course.' She pointed to the phone.

Quickly Mandy went and dialled the number, urging her mother to hurry and pick up the phone. 'Mum, it's me. I'm at Spillers'. Dad's gone missing in the snow. We're sending out a search-party.' She spoke in a rush, then stopped short. There was a long pause. 'Mum, are you there?'

'Yes, Mandy. I got all that. I'll run down to Grandad at the village hall and get him to drive me straight up. Don't worry, we'll find him. Your dad knows what to do in these situations. We'll

soon have him back safe and sound.' Emily Hope
rang off.

Mandy put down the phone. She felt less afraid.
Her mum's calm voice was a huge help. Now she
passed on the message to Mrs Spiller. 'Mum will try
to get up here with Grandad. Can you watch out for
them, please?' She rushed to the door to follow Mr
Western's search-party.

'Don't split up,' he was telling the group as they
emerged into the freezing white air. 'Stick together.
Dennis will have to lead the way. Come on!'
Together they tramped out on to the tractor track,
heads down, forming a tight bunch as they set off
up the hill.

Mandy settled into the pace, steady but slow
through the soft snow. She wore her scarf wrapped
high round her face, but still the freezing wind tore
through her and the snowflakes blinded her. Beside
her, James struggled to lift his legs clear of the snow
with each wearying step.

Up ahead, Dennis came to a halt. 'I think it's this
way now.' They cut off to the left, like Arctic
explorers, into a wilderness that no one recognised.

For a few more minutes they trekked over the
uneven ground. Mandy stepped to her waist into a
snow-covered hollow.

James hauled her out. 'We must be nearly there!' he gasped.

But Dennis had hesitated a second time. 'I was sure it was this way!' He searched all round for landmarks, but covered in snow, the terrain was strange and unfamiliar. The group scanned the hillside without seeing any sign of Adam Hope and the sheep.

'Try shouting!' Sam Western suggested.

The call went up in every direction. They cupped gloved hands to their mouths and shouted for the vet. But the snow deadened their cries, and there was no reply.

Dennis Saville shook his head. He turned to Dean. 'Which way now?'

'It all looks different: I couldn't say.'

'And how long has he been out in this now?' Dora Janeki asked. She looked grim, as if she knew there was a limit to what a person lost in the snow could stand.

'About an hour and a half,' Jack Spiller said.

Mandy scoured the snowy slopes for signs of her father; footsteps, a half-covered trail. But the snow drifted as it landed and wiped away all tracks. She felt a hopelessness settle on them. 'Dad!' she called out. The hillside threw back a dead, muffled silence.

She looked desperately at James.

'Well, this is no good. I suggest we go back to the house,' Sam Western decided. 'We've gone wrong somehow. It's no one's fault. Conditions up here are terrible. We'd better get on the phone to the rescue service and fetch them up as quick as we can.'

He turned and led them down the hill, using his mobile phone to call for paramedics and the police. They had to guess their way back to Jack Spiller's place, arriving weary and downhearted as Mrs Spiller threw open the door to great them.

'We can't find him!' Mandy ran the last few metres and dashed into the kitchen. 'Is Mum here yet?'

'No. No one's got through so far.' Mrs Spiller had hot tea and stiff drinks waiting.

Jack told his wife that the police were sending a rescue vehicle from Walton. The police realised it was an emergency; a man missing on the moor in this weather. They would pull out all the stops.

But the waiting was dreadful for Mandy. She stood with James out in the porch, straining to hear the sound of a car engine, longing for her mum to arrive. She looked for headlights in the snow, imagining them and then feeling her hopes die. At last, she caught a sound and struggled out into the snow, across the yard to the gate. Sure enough, her grandad's camper van came crawling up the hill, skidding sideways, its back wheels sliding and kicking up snow.

Mandy ran down the hill. Her mum jumped out of the van, dressed in a tough blue jacket and boots. Grandad braked into the side of the road and turned off the lights. He ran to join them.

'Oh, Mum, hurry!' Mandy cried. 'We can't find him. The snow's too bad. He's lost!'

Emily Hope nodded. 'OK, keep calm. Which way?' She turned to Mr Hope. 'Let's take another look.'

'This way! We went up with the first search-party, but we all got lost.' She waded into a drift, towards the two stone walls that showed the line of the tractor track. They were still just visible under the snow. She wondered how her mum could stay so calm.

They all set their faces against a headwind and struggled on. 'Here!' James came to the end of the tractor track. 'This is where we found the first sheep, remember!' This time he felt they were on the right track. 'And Mr Hope headed up that way to the second sheep!'

Mandy nodded. She felt a flicker of hope. But, as they sank waist-deep into more drifts, she grew desperate again. She heard Grandad begin to shout

out his son's name. Snow whirled down without end. Still they pressed on.

Then Mandy stopped. She thought she heard a low whine. She told herself that it was impossible, but she peered through the storm. 'Wait a minute, Grandad! Did you hear that?'

There was another whine, coming nearer, and a bark.

'Tess!' Mandy would have recognised the sound anywhere. 'Here, girl!' They stood, fixed to the spot, waiting for her to appear.

A shape scrambled down the hill. It was Tess. Her dark coat was matted with frozen snow, but her brown eyes were alert, her tail carried high. She bounded towards Mandy, who fell to the ground to hug her.

Grandad, James and Emily Hope came crowding round. 'Good girl!' James told her. 'At least we can take you back with us this time!' He told Mrs Hope the story of who had really attacked the sheep.

'Hold back a minute; it looks like she wants us to follow, not the other way round!' Grandad pulled Mandy to her feet and stood looking at Tess. The dog barked and ran up the hill a little way. Then she came back and barked again. She looked up at Mandy, darted away, and came back.

'She does!' Mandy could see she wanted to show them something.

Straight away they set off after Tess, treading deep into new snow, only waiting when Tess stopped to listen, ears pricked. Then she dashed forward again, impatient for them to follow.

'Is she up to what I think she's up to?' Grandad asked. 'Is she trying to show us where Adam is?'

Mandy looked at her mum and grandad and nodded. 'I'm sure that's what she's doing!' She ploughed ahead, with James at her side.

'What do you think?' Mandy's grandad asked Emily Hope.

'I think we should trust her.'

Mandy heard them hurry to catch up. 'Go on, Tess! Show us the way. Good girl!' Still the dog struggled shoulder-deep through the snow, looking, listening. She answered a signal with a sharp bark and a swift change of direction.

'What was that? I didn't hear anything!' James said.

'No, but Tess did. Come on!' Mandy would have trusted her to the ends of the earth.

At last, after what seemed like an age Tess came to a steep dip. It ran twenty metres to a row of beech trees beside a frozen stream. Tess waited for them, then bounded down the slope.

'Listen!' Mandy said. 'I heard a whistle!'

James nodded. They ran after Tess, half-tumbling, skidding and sliding down the hill. 'Where, Tess? Where is he? Show us, girl!'

Snow had drifted against the trees in white mounds that came shoulder-high. Tess was light, able to leap from mound to mound. The whistle grew louder.

'Dad!' Mandy called. She strained to see through the snowflakes. 'Dad, where are you?'

There was a faint shout. 'Here!'

Mandy shouted back. 'Oh, Dad, thank heavens!' She turned to her mum and grandad. 'He's alive!' They came running down the hill. 'Hang on, Dad! Tess is trying to find you. Whistle again!' She watched as Tess began to scrape with her front paws at the side of the furthest drift.

'Here!' Mandy heard her dad's muffled voice again. She and James scrambled to the far side of the drift and dropped on to their knees. They saw a deep tunnel scooped into the snow. Mandy leaned inside. She found the huddled shape of her father waiting patiently for rescue.

Tess bounded up the slope and barked out their success. The others came running. Emily Hope fell to the ground and wriggled into the snow hole

to check Adam's condition. There were tears in her eyes as she crawled back out. 'Let's lift him out,' she said. 'I think he's going to be all right, but we'll have to go carefully.'

Gently they lifted Mandy's father out of the shelter he'd dug into the snow. He was stiff and numb. Snow had frozen into his beard, he couldn't feel his feet, his legs could scarcely stand.

'Don't forget the sheep,' he told them. 'Try and pull her out as well.'

Grandad and James dug deep into the tunnel. They scraped the snow out until they found the animal. She was still alive.

'We'll have to carry her down to Jack's place,' Adam Hope insisted. He staggered and tried to stand.

'*You* won't be carrying anyone,' Emily Hope told him. She watched as Mandy helped to steady him and slung his arm round her shoulder. 'You'll have enough trouble carrying yourself down. Here, let me help.'

Mandy looked up at her dad, tears in her eyes. 'Can you walk?' she whispered.

He nodded and found his balance.

'We'll bring the sheep,' James said. He and Mandy's grandad began to work out how they should carry her. Emily Hope took her husband's hand and began to lead him up the slope.

Mandy stayed behind for a moment with Tess, by the snow hole that had stopped her father from freezing to death. 'You saved his life,' she whispered in the dog's soft ear. She tried to wipe the snow from her back. 'You're a brilliant dog, and now everyone knows it!' She spoke gently. 'There's no danger now, Tess. You can come back with us.' She got to her feet and walked a couple of paces up the hill. 'Come on, girl!'

But Tess had completed her task. She'd saved Adam Hope's life. Now she turned away from Mandy and began to tread lightly up the opposite slope.

'Tess, here girl!'

The dog didn't falter. She walked on, up the hill towards High Cross, without looking back.

Mandy watched her go. How could Tess know that it was safe to come back? She wished she could make her understand. She wished dogs knew human words. She longed to take her home.

But Mandy watched in silence as Tess reached the top of the ridge. The clouds lifted now, the snow began to clear. Mandy could follow Tess's lonely shape along the white horizon. She didn't call again.

With a sad heart she turned to follow her father,

her mother, Grandad and James. The dog who'd saved many lives was a stray again. She was homeless on Christmas Eve, wandering the snowy hills.

Twelve

'Tess certainly saved us a hard job!' the paramedic told Mandy. They'd arrived just in time to see Adam Hope being brought off the hillside by members of his own family. All the rescue team needed to do was to check that he wouldn't suffer any long-term effects from his afternoon in the snow. 'That dog of yours must be some kind of heroine!'

Mandy had told him all about Tess; how her sharp hearing had picked up Mr Hope's whistle, how she'd come to find them and show them the way. She stood by as the rescue team led her dad into the ambulance and insisted on seeing him safely home.

Sam Western and his group of rescuers stood at

the Spillers' gate, watching them go. All had ended well. Both sheep would recover, thanks to Adam Hope. And Mr Western had taken the blame squarely on his own shoulders.

Dora Janeki came forward to tell Mandy how she felt. 'I'd take Tess back straight away if I could.' They watched Emily Hope climb up into the ambulance and the doors close. 'We'd have to go a long way to find another dog like that!'

Mandy nodded. But she said nothing. The truth had come out too late to save Tess.

'I really am sorry.' Dora patted Mandy's shoulder and walked away.

'Come on, you two!' Grandad came and told James and Mandy to jump into the camper van. 'Let's follow the ambulance. We can go and tell your gran that everyone's safe.'

So they left the moorside, still deep in snow. The storm had died as quickly as it had come, and the skies were clear. The afternoon was ending in pale sunlight which sparkled along the hilltop.

They went home to Welford. Mrs Hunter met James in the village and took him back to their house. Gran stood waiting anxiously outside the village hall. She watched the ambulance drive past with Adam and Emily safe inside. Grandad stopped the van for her to climb in. 'Don't worry, everyone's fine!' he told her.

Gran took a deep breath. 'Of course everyone's fine!' she said. 'I warned you not to make a fuss. Adam knows what he's doing.' She turned to smile at Mandy. 'We Hopes are a tough lot!'

Mandy was secretly glad that Gran hadn't been out in that blizzard. No matter how tough the Hopes were, she knew her dad wouldn't have survived much longer.

'And . . .' Gran announced proudly as they followed the ambulance up the drive to Animal Ark '. . . everything's ready for the party! We went ahead and got the food across to the hall. It's all laid on, ready and waiting!'

'Gran, are you sure?' Mandy slid open the side door and jumped down into half a metre of crunchy snow. 'I thought we might have to cancel it after all this!'

Gran stepped down and stood, hands on hips. 'Cancel! Just because of a little snowstorm?' She made it sound like a ridiculous idea. 'Whoever heard of a drop of snow stopping us from enjoying ourselves at Christmas?'

Slowly Mandy's face broke into a smile. She went up and hugged her gran, letting a quiet tear fall for

Tess, who wouldn't be there to join in the fun.

'There, that's better,' Gran said gently. 'Now, dry your eyes and get yourself into the party spirit. In spite of everything, I have a feeling that this is going to be the best Christmas Eve you can ever remember!'

The snow ploughs drove out from Walton to clear the main roads. Farmers brought out their tractors and broke a way through from the high farms down to the village. Snow lay heaped against the walls in white banks that dwarfed the cars as they came down to the village for the candlelit gathering at the Fox and Goose.

Mandy arrived just before half past seven. Mrs Ponsonby was already there with Pandora and Toby. Pandora was decked out in a Christmas ribbon tied round her neck in an enormous bow. John Hardy came out with Button and Barney warmly snuggled inside a spare cat basket. He wore a pirate's hat and an eyepatch, to the amusement of little Claire McKay, who had just turned up with James's Blackie. She wore a cardboard crown covered in gold foil, with rubies and diamonds made of shiny boiled sweets stuck on round the rim. Everyone laughed and chattered. Gran arrived with a tray of candles stuck into oranges, decorated with spices, sweets and red ribbon. She began to light them and hand them round. The party was about to begin.

Mandy took a peep inside her jacket at Mopsy, the favourite of her three pet rabbits, curled up safe and warm inside a specially made sling. Her ears twitched. Her sleepy eyes blinked back at Mandy.

'Hi, Brandon!' Claire and Blackie ran to meet the latest arrivals. Mrs Gill had dropped Brandon and Ruby the pig in the pub carpark. Ruby was wearing the party-hat; a battered straw trilby decorated with plastic sunflowers. Brandon picked her up as she made a beeline for Pandora's shiny bow. 'Behave yourself,' he warned, red with embarrassment.

Mandy knew that Grandad had driven the van up on to the moor again to fetch Lydia and Houdini. He brought them now, with young Jenny Spiller and her sheep. The door opened and they tumbled out into the snowy yard, nosy and excited. Houdini kicked up his heels, ready to make a break. 'Steady, boy!' Lydia warned. She held him back. 'I expect he's looking for something to eat,' she explained.

Soon Walter Pickard came out of the pub with old Tom, his chewed ear ragged but nicely healed. Ernie Bell followed with Sammy, proudly producing his cap from his pocket and pinning a sprig of mistletoe to the side. He put it on his grey, stubbly head. 'You never know your luck!' he grinned. He and Lydia got ready to join the procession together.

'Where's James?' Mandy looked round the glowing group. She took a christingle candle from her gran. 'He should be here by now.'

Gran looked mysterious. 'I expect Eric is playing up. Maybe James has had to stop and look for him.'

'Oh, but hadn't we better wait for them?' Mandy didn't want to start without James.

'We could go ahead,' Gran said. 'I'm sure he wouldn't mind!'

Mandy frowned. It wasn't like James to be late for something so important.

Next Andi Greenaway turned up from Manor Farm. She led Dorian along the main street. The old donkey stepped sturdily through the snow, his large, flat feet plodding softly, his nose poking over all the garden gates as he came along. Andi was dressed in an old striped blanket, with a tea-towel tied round her head, carrying a shepherd's crook in her hand. 'I'm a Christmas shepherd,' she told Brandon and John. 'Anyone can see that!'

But the star turn was Susan Price with Prince. She arrived five minutes late, riding tall in a red sombrero hat. Her wide brim was laden with fake oranges, bananas, pineapples and grapes. Prince wore one to match, with holes cut in the crown for his ears, the brim tilted at a jaunty angle. Susan wore a Spanish guitar slung across her shoulder, and a silvery shirt covered in frills and ruffles.

'Oh, my!' Mrs Ponsonby cried, as Pandora ran yapping towards the late arrivals.

Dorian and Ruby wandered across to investigate the fruit. The little pig snorted and snuffled. Dorian backed off, disappointed to find that the pineapples were plastic. Susan laughed. 'Sorry I'm late!' she called.

'Ready?' Mrs Ponsonby scooped Pandora into her arms and called Toby to her. She formed them into a procession and struck up the first carol.

Good King Wenceslas looked out
On the Feast of Stephen . . .

She stood at the head of the queue, hitting a lively rhythm. Soon the others joined in.

'Don't worry about James,' Gran winked at Mandy. 'He'll soon catch up!'

The procession was on the move. Mandy stood holding her candle, waiting until the last minute.

She gazed down the road for any sign of her best friend.

'Come on, Mandy!' Mrs Ponsonby urged from up front.

So Mandy joined them, breaking into song.

> *. . . Brightly shone the moon that night,*
> *Though the frost was cruel,*
> *When a poor man came in sight,*
> *Gathering winter fu-u-el!*

It was a lovely sight; the long, candlelit procession trailing down the snow-covered street. The sound of music rang out, the stars shone down from a clear sky. People came to their doors to smile and join in with the Christmas spirit. The guests slowly made their way; pets and owners, all shapes and sizes, ages, colours; all part of the magical event.

Mrs Ponsonby drew them to a halt outside the porch of the village hall. Everyone stood round in a semicircle to finish their song.

'Come on, Mandy,' Gran whispered, taking her by the arm and leading her forward.

'What's going on?' Mandy found herself surrounded by smiling faces lit by soft, yellow candlelight. She was gently drawn to the front. Sammy the squirrel

darted on to her shoulder and ran chattering up and down her arm. Then he sat perched, his tail brushing her cheek.

'Go ahead.' Mrs Ponsonby stepped aside with a gracious gesture. 'This is *your* party, Mandy. Without you, none of this would have happened!'

Mandy took a deep, deep breath. She delved inside her jacket to take Mopsy out of the sling she'd made to cradle him. Sammy still sat jauntily on her shoulder. She handed her candle to Ernie and kicked the snow off her boots. Then she stepped into the porch and opened the door.

Inside the brilliantly lit hall, her mum and dad stood waiting to greet her. Mum's red hair was swept on to the top of her head. She wore her best blue party dress and smiled happily. Dad, showered and spruced up, and none the worse for his ordeal, stood with his arm around his wife's waist.

Beyond them, all Mandy could see through her happy tears was a riot of coloured balloons, streamers, holly, Christmas lights and the tall green tree. She smelt hot fruit punch, heard festive music drifting from the loudspeakers. The lights seemed to float and swim. The whole room was alive.

Then she saw James walking towards her, carrying Eric. She felt the other guests jostle her forward.

She heard Gran whisper in her ear. 'Look, Mandy. Look who James has brought!'

James grinned as he gave a command. 'Sit, girl! Tess, sit!'

Mandy stared down at his feet.

Tess sat looking back at her with her liquid brown eyes. Someone had brushed her coat to a smooth, glossy shine. Her white chest and the white stripe down her muzzle gleamed. At the sight of Mandy, her tail swept the floor, back and forth.

'Tess!' Mandy felt Sammy jump from her shoulder in surprise. She handed Mopsy to her gran. Then she went forward to touch the dog, to make it real, so that she wouldn't wake up and find this all a dream. She ran her hand down Tess's neck and patted her shoulder. 'Is it really you?' she breathed.

Tess growled softly. Then Ruby came in and broke them apart with her little hard trotters and soft snout. She buffeted Tess out of the way, heading straight for the nearest food.

'Where . . . ? How . . . ? When? The questions tumbled out as the party began.

James explained everything. He'd persuaded his mother to take him back up to High Cross before it got dark. Ken Hudson had spotted him and agreed to help find Tess. They knew which way she'd headed after the rescue. They had found Tess's trail by the Celtic cross and began to call her name. Lydia came out of her house and said she'd seen a dog in the woods at the back of the farm. James and Ken ran to find her curled up in an exhausted sleep in the shelter of a tumbledown wall. Ken had put her on a lead and they took her back to Dora's, who soon set her right with food and good care. Ken had brought Tess down to the village in time for James to bring her to the party in secret.

'I wanted it to be a surprise for you!' he said.

'It was!' Mandy felt her heart swell. 'It's perfect! It's everything I ever wished! Thank you, James. Oh, thank you!'

'So Tess is the guest of honour?' Grandad stepped carefully between cats and dogs to come and speak to them. 'I'm glad everything's worked out fine.'

Mandy smiled. She sat with Tess at her feet as Mrs Ponsonby organised the competition. She awarded the party-hat prize to Prince and Susan just before Houdini snatched a bite at the pony's felt sombrero. Then Simon played more music, the pets got their party food, and the people too were fed. Gran brought hot mince-pies from the small kitchen – Pandora disgraced herself over the sausage-rolls.

All in all, the party was a great success. Everyone

agreed that the pets behaved perfectly – even Mrs Ponsonby said so!

'Of course!' Mandy said to James. She still sat with one arm round Tess's neck.

He smiled at her. She smiled back. They'd made it. Everyone was safe, Tess had a home, the pets were at their party. 'Happy Christmas, James!' she said. 'A very, very happy Christmas!'

Read more about Animal Ark in
Lamb in the Laundry

One

'Ready?' said Mr Hope.

'Just coming,' Mandy replied, smiling at her dad. 'Blackie wants to carry the picnic basket.'

Mr Hope grinned. 'So long as he doesn't eat all the food,' he said.

'Even Blackie couldn't manage all that,' said James. He pushed his glasses up his nose and bent down to Blackie. Blackie was James's Labrador. 'Put it down, Blackie,' he said.

Blackie looked up at him and wagged his tail – but he held on to the handle of the basket.

Mandy laughed. 'He isn't getting any more obedient,' she said.

James shoved his hair out of his eyes. 'Down, Blackie!' he said.

Blackie looked up at James sorrowfully and barked. The basket tumbled to the ground.

'Got it,' Mandy said, snatching it up. She looked at Blackie. 'You'll get your share of the picnic, Blackie,' she said.

'Lucky there isn't anything breakable in there,' said Mrs Hope.

Mandy looked at her mum, leaning through the kitchen window of the cottage.

'It's a wonder he could pick it up,' she said. 'What have you put in here, Mum?'

Emily Hope laughed and her green eyes danced. Her red hair shone in the sun. 'Oh, this and that,' she said. 'Enough to keep three hungry people happy.'

'And a hungry dog,' James said, grabbing Blackie's collar before he could get to the basket again.

'Enough for a siege,' said Mr Hope as he got into the car. 'Come on then. We haven't got all day.'

Mrs Hope laughed. 'But that's exactly what you have got,' she said. 'A whole day to ramble on the moors and have a picnic.'

Mandy turned to her mother. 'It's a pity you can't come, Mum,' she said.

Emily Hope shook her head. 'Somebody has to mind the surgery,' she said. 'And it's ages since your dad had a day off.'

'And I'm going to make the most of it,' Adam Hope said. 'Get in, you two – three,' he added, looking at Blackie.

Mandy and James got into the car. Blackie bounded after them.

'Have a good time,' Mrs Hope called.

Jean Knox, the surgery receptionist, appeared at the window beside her. 'Enjoy yourselves,' she said.

Mandy looked back as the car drove out of Animal Ark's driveway. Mrs Hope and Jean waved from the kitchen window. It was a lovely sunny morning and Mandy wished her mum could have come with them. She sighed.

Mr Hope turned his head. 'Someone has to look after the animals,' he said.

Mandy nodded. Animal Ark was a busy veterinary practice and both her parents were vets. They didn't have much free time. And Mum was right: it had been ages since Mr Hope had had a day off.

'It's going to be wonderful,' Mandy said.

Mr Hope laughed. 'That's the spirit!' he said. 'I'm looking forward to this picnic.'

'So is Blackie,' James said.

Mandy gave the Labrador a hug. 'First you have to do a bit of walking,' Mandy said. 'Then we eat.'

Blackie wagged his tail and knocked James's glasses off.

'Blackie!' said James, laughing.

Blackie wasn't the most obedient dog in the world – or the best behaved – but he was great fun.

'Where are we going?' James said as he settled his glasses back on his nose.

Mandy turned round to point out of the car window to the moor above Welford village. 'Up there,' she said. 'Black Tor.'

'Terrific,' said James. 'It's ages since I've been up to Black Tor.'

The car swung round the crossroads by the Fox and Goose pub and Mandy and James waved to Mr Hardy, the publican, as they passed. He looked up from rolling a barrel into the pub and waved back.

Then they were out of the village and climbing towards the moor. Mandy loved the moor. It could be wild and windy in winter and the snow could pile itself into drifts two metres deep. But today, in the spring sunshine, it looked perfect.

The car climbed higher and Mandy and James looked back. Welford lay spread out below them. They could see Animal Ark, the old stone cottage at the front and the modern extension that housed the surgery at the back. They spotted James's house at the other end of the village and Mandy's grandparents' cottage with their camper van sitting outside. And behind the Fox and Goose was the lane where Walter Pickard and Ernie Bell lived, both church bell-ringers like Grandad. Then there was the church and the post office and the village hall.

'It looks like a toy village,' James said.

'Look,' said Mandy. 'You can see Walton. There's the school.' Walton was the neighbouring town, two miles from Welford.

'Ugh!' groaned James. 'Don't mention school. Not when the holidays have just begun!'

'And there's the cottage hospital,' Mandy said, pointing to a long, low building on the outskirts of Walton. It was the little local hospital for Walton and Welford. 'Gran says there's a new matron there now.'

If you like *Animal Ark*® then you'll love *Animal Action*!
Subscribe for just **£8** and you can look forward to six
issues of *Animal Action* magazine, throughout the year.
Each issue of *Animal Action* is bursting with animal
news and features, competitions and fun and games! Plus,
when you subscribe, you'll become a free *Animal Action*
Club member too, so we'll send you a fab joining pack
and FREE donkey notepad and pen!

To subscribe, simply complete the form below – a photocopy is fine – and send it with a
cheque for £8 (made payable to RSPCA) to RSPCA Animal Action Club, Wilberforce Way,
Southwater, Horsham, West Sussex RH13 9RS.

Don't delay, join today!

Name:

Address:

Postcode:	Date of birth:

Signature of parent/guardian:

Data Protection Act: This information will be held on computer and used only by the RSPCA.
Please allow 28 days for delivery. **AACHOD07**